HEALED BY THE EARTH DRAGON PRINCE

ARIA WINTER

JADE WALTZ

Purple Fall
Publishing

Published in the United States by Purple Fall Publishing. Purple Fall Publishing and the Purple Fall Publishing Logos are trademarks and/or registered trademarks of Purple Fall Publishing LLC.

Publisher's Cataloging-in-Publication data

Names: Winter, Aria, author. | Waltz, Jade, author.

Title: Healed By The Earth Dragon Prince / Aria Winter & Jade Waltz.

Series: Elemental Dragon Warriors

Description: Purple Fall Publishing, 2021.

Identifiers: ISBN:

978-1-64253-298-2 (pbk.)

978-1-64253-242-5 (ebook)

978-1-64253-476-4 (audiobook)

Subjects: LCSH Space exploration--Fiction. | Human-alien encounters--Fiction. | Dragons--Fiction. | Shapeshifting--Fiction. | Science fiction. | Romance fiction. | BISAC FICTION / Science Fiction / Alien Contact | FICTION / Romance / Science Fiction | FICTION / Romance / Paranormal / Shifters

Classification: LCC PS3623 .I6675 H43 2021 | DDC 813.6--dc23

Cover Design: Kim Cunningham of Atlantis Book Design

PRINTED IN THE UNITED STATES OF AMERICA

Dedication

To my husband: Thank you for all your love and support. You are not just my husband, you are my best friend and my rock. I love you more than anything.

-Aria Winter

To My Husband,
Thank you for being my support and rock during this writing journey. I love you!

-Jade Waltz

CHAPTER 1

ANNA

Sirens blare and red lights flash across the corridors as we race through the ship. Terrified screams echo behind us. I wrap my arm tighter around Jarod's waist as he leans heavily against me, dragging him toward the escape pods. His breathing is ragged as he tries to keep up. His arm around my shoulders grows heavier with each step. Normally, I wouldn't dare move a patient with such a severe injury, but I don't have a choice. I refuse to leave him behind.

"Leave me," he rasps. "I'm not going to make it."

"Don't give up now," I tell him, not bothering to slow down. "We're almost there."

An inhuman roar fills the air. The alien pirates have forced their way onto the ship. A blast of light zips past us, hitting the panel next to my head.

"Hurry!" a woman wails. "They're coming!"

I look over my shoulder and gasp when yellow eyes with vertically slit pupils meet mine. Covered from head to toe in light-green scales, the alien raises his blaster and fires off a shot. The world *shifts into slow-motion as light erupts from the barrel and races toward us.*

Jared slams into my side, pushing me back against the wall and out of the path of the shot. I watch the blast hit Jarod square in the chest, horrified. He cries out and goes silent, crumpling to the floor.

"No!" I fall to my knees and lean over him, pressing my hands to his chest as if I can somehow stop the bleeding.

His eyes are wide and unfocused. He takes my hand weakly in his. "Go," he barely manages.

Still in shock, I reach down and brush a lock of white hair from his brow, the blood on my hands streaking red through the strands. I cannot speak through my tears. Someone approaches to my right and I look up just in time to see the alien aim the blaster at Jarod's head and fire.

"No!"

"Anna!" Holly's voice rips me from my sleep. I jerk upright in bed and place my hand on my chest, trying to calm my pounding heart. Drawing in a deep breath, I look at my friend.

"I'm sorry I woke you," she murmurs, "but you were having a nightmare. Are you all right?"

When I close my eyes, an image of Jarod's lifeless form fills my mind. He was like a father to me after my parents died. I'll never be all right again.

"Yeah," I lie. "I'm fine. It was just a dream."

I brush my long chestnut hair back from my face and throw my legs over the side of the bed. I hate this. Ever since alien pirates attacked our colony ships, there have been very few nights that I don't relive the experience in my nightmares.

I pull on my long green robes. My friend Lilly gave them to me yesterday. She picked out this fabric for me because she said it matched my eyes. As I gaze at myself in the mirror, I believe she is right.

I glance around the room. The deep-orange and crimson brick walls of the apartment are a welcome sight, reminding me that we've left the colony ships behind. Ever since the Drakarians—the dragon-shifter aliens who inhabit this planet—of the Fire Clan found us in the desert, they've been nothing but kind, going out of their way to help us settle in their capital city, Valoria.

My friend Lilliana is now married—I mean, *mated*—to Prince Varus of the Fire Clan. I've spent enough time around them to see what a great guy she picked. He practically worships the ground that she walks on. When these Drakarians fall for someone, they fall hard.

Varus found Lilly when we were still in the desert. She had ventured from camp to scout for shelter. The moment he saw her, he recognized her as his fated mate. Everywhere they go, Prince Varus proudly displays the glowing fate mark on his chest. An indication that she is, in fact, his fated one—or *linaya*, as they call it.

A plague swept through this world a few years ago and killed the majority of Drakarian women. Many of those who survived were left barren. Now that Lilly is pregnant with Varus's child, the remaining Drakarian men are desperate to court a human, hoping to entice us to bond with them.

Holly smiles. "I'm going to work now. I'll see you when I get back tonight. Say hi to Lilly for me, all right?"

Holly was a teacher on the ships. She's been working hard to learn everything she can about Drakarian teaching methods, hoping to get a permanent position at one of the schools here.

My friend, Lilly, is a botanist and she's been collaborating with her Drakarian counterparts to incorporate some of our Earth seeds into next season's crops.

Each of us is trying to find our way in this new world. I was one of the ship's doctors—the only one who made it onto our escape pod. I've been working with Healer Ranas to learn how they practice medicine here.

The Drakarians are searching both in space and across their planet for any other escape pods and survivors, but so far, we've found none.

"All right," I give her my best grin, feigning a carefree attitude. "I'll see you later."

As soon as she leaves, I gather my things and head out the door. I'm supposed to meet Lilly for breakfast this morning; I hope she won't try to set me up again.

Apparently one of the Fire Clan guards likes me. He's nice and all, but I'm not interested in a boyfriend just yet. I'm still getting settled. Besides, he didn't display a glowing mark on his chest to tell him that I'm his *linaya,* and even if he did, I'm not ready to date him. Not after what happened with Edward.

As I make my way to the castle, I consider how much I've learned about medicine in my short time here. Frustratingly, most Drakarian Healers come from the Earth Clan and possess the ability to breathe healing fire. All they have to do is blow blue-green flame on a wound and the tissue heals before your eyes. It's amazing, but I'll never be able to match their skill.

Still, there are other ways I can be useful. Their healing fire cannot replace blood loss, cleanse someone of toxins, or eradicate pathogens from the body. For those things, simple medicine, instead of healing fire, are called for. And that's something I can definitely use my skills to do.

As I walk up the path toward the castle, a Drakarian man smiles brightly at me. "Would you like me to fly you to your destination?"

I return the smile at his nice offer. Until we can add human-friendly modifications to the city, the Drakarians are always eager to fly us where we need to go. Since they have wings, their city isn't easily navigable for us wingless humans. But several of their engineers are working on bridges and lifts even now.

It's nice here, I just wish there was more vegetation. The forested mountains and jungles of old Earth were always my favorite places to explore in the virtual reality rooms on the ships. I'm not going to complain though because the Fire Clan people have been good to us since they've taken us in.

The city itself is surrounded by a desert. Our apartments are located at the top of a mesa, close to the castle. Each building is colored in shades of red like the sand, clay, and rock they are built from, including the palace. I marvel again at the gold-capped domes of the four corner towers of the castle, shining like beautiful jewels beneath the red-orange sun.

The ice-blue sky is clear except for a few thin wisps of gray clouds, but the air is cool and bone dry, without even the tiniest hint of moisture.

More city districts are carved into the mesa walls, only accessible by flying. A sparkling river winds around the base and feeds water into the crop fields. The verdant green vegetation stands in sharp contrast to the fire-red rocks and sand that surround the farms.

Across the way lies a plateau with more housing dotting the cliff wall. Beyond that stretches an expanse of crimson sand, punctuated by towering rock formations.

"Thank you," I tell the friendly Drakarian. "I think I'll take you up on that."

His smile widens. Despite their alien appearance, I can't deny most Drakarian men are handsome. Each Clan has a unique color variation on their bodies. The Fire Clan dragons have red-and-orange scales.

I shudder inwardly as I think of the Wind Clan. I haven't met them yet, but John has. He was with my friend Skye when she was taken by a Wind dragon. From the description John gave—light-gray scales, white horns, and a long scar down the left side of his face—Varus says it was Prince Raidyn who took her. He swears up and down that no Drakarian, regardless of Clan, would ever harm a female. But if that's the case, why did that prince abduct her?

That's what unsettles me. I'd like to think these guys would never force us to bond with them, but the fact that my friend Skye is still missing gives me pause.

The Fire Clan Drakarian's orange-rimmed, reptilian pupils contract and expand as he eyes me appraisingly. Proud black horns spiral up from his head, only adding to his impressive height. He smiles, baring a row of sharp fangs, but I don't find them terrifying anymore. The sharp, lethal black claws that tip his fingers don't intimidate me either.

The one thing that does make me a bit uncomfortable is the nudity. Their people think nothing of walking around without a single stitch of clothing. Some wear robes, but most wear nothing since they are so used to shifting forms. At least their private parts are concealed in a mating pouch, so they're not flashing anyone.

"Would you like me to carry you in this form or my *draka* form?" he asks with a roguishly handsome grin.

Their *draka* form is several times the size of their humanoid form and looks like a medieval dragon from a legend. It still scares me a bit. "This form is fine."

A deafening roar splits the air and my gaze snaps toward the sky. Panic races through me when I notice over a dozen dragons flying toward the city. Their white and gray scales shimmer iridescently beneath the red-orange sun. Panic stills my heart. That coloring means they come from the Wind Clan—the dragons who stole Skye.

"Run. Hide," the Fire dragon tells me. I freeze as he transforms in a whirl of dust and wind into *draka* form, turning into a massive crimson dragon before my eyes. He looks down at me again. "Go. Quickly!"

He spreads his large wings and lifts into the sky, racing to meet the Wind Clan invaders head-on.

Sirens blare throughout the city, muffling the sounds of terrified cries and screams as people rush to find cover.

Stunned, I watch as Fire and Wind *draka* collide in a rage of teeth and claws above our heads, raining obsidian blood as they tear into one another. Buildings crumble and explode where they crash down, showering chunks of rock and debris onto the streets.

Complete chaos erupts as people scatter in all directions, searching for a place to hide. A gust of air behind me pushes me forward, nearly knocking me down. I brace myself against a nearby wall. A bellow sounds overhead, so close the sound vibrates through my body. I turn to meet massive, green eyes with elongated pupils. A scream bursts from my lungs when a large, taloned hand covered in gray scales wraps around my body, ripping me into the sky.

My long brown hair whips around my head, obscuring my vision as I thrash and beat my fists against the Wind dragon's hold, desperate to escape. A blur of red in the corner of my eye draws my attention, and I turn just as a Fire dragon rams into the side of my captor.

The Wind draka roars loudly, and we begin a tight, spiraling fall. The ground races toward us with dizzying speed. At the last second, his wings snap open, halting our descent only a few feet above the ground. Another dragon attacks, lashing out with his claws and tearing into his flesh.

He relinquishes his grip on my form and I drop the last few feet to the ground. The air is forced from my lungs as I slam against the stone walkway, flat on my back. The world shifts into slow motion as I stare up at the sky, dazed and gasping for air. My ears are still ringing from the drop and everything sounds muffled all around me. I know I should get up, but I cannot make myself move. Not yet.

A deafening *boom* splits the air overhead and time speeds up as another dragon crashes into the wall beside me. An explosion of dust and debris rains down from the impact. Blinding pain rips through my side and the sharp *snap* of breaking bone fills my ears as a rock hits my torso. Despite my injury, I force myself to stand, bracing one arm against my ribcage.

Two dragons, white and red, fight above me. A long, white tail whips out, smashing into what's left of the wall nearby. I jump away too late. Something hits the back of my head and my world goes dark.

CHAPTER 2

KAJ

I stand on my balcony, surveying the mountains and the vast forest below. I leave tomorrow for Fire Clan territory, though I am loath to return to the desert plains. The dry air and crimson sands are a barren wasteland compared to my Clan's territory. I don't know how their people manage to live in such a place.

The Fire Clan territory is as different to Earth Clan territory as night is to day. Varus's castle sits atop a mesa that looks out upon a great desert beyond. But here, our castle is built into the side of a mountain, surrounded by dense vegetation. All of the various houses and residences are carved into the mountains around us.

Drakarians in two-legged and draka form fly overhead as they go about their day. Many of them are preparing for the flower festival. It is still a few cycles away, but it is always a large enough event that they take much time with their preparations.

The air is slightly humid from the constant rains we've

had these past few weeks and I inhale deeply, appreciating the strong and earthy scents of the forest. When I look off to the side, I notice several of the vines that climb up the castle walls are already dotted with small buds, readying to bloom within the next few weeks.

I have visited all the various territories of this world, but nothing compares to our territory here. Perhaps I am biased, but I feel that none can rival the untamed and raw beauty of Earth Clan lands.

I lift my cup to my lips and inhale the steam of my valo tea. I take a sip, savoring the warm liquid that rolls across my tongue. With a sweet tang of citrus, berry, and just a hint of spice, this is the best blend of the season so far. I must make a batch for my friend, Prince Varus. The blend he usually drinks is so bitter, I don't know how he stands the taste.

However, I never did enjoy tea before he introduced me to valo. He would always bring a mix when he and his sister came to visit. We'd sit together for hours on end playing narku on the balcony while we sipped at our drinks.

Then the plague swept through our world, taking his older sister and mine. Varus came to visit me then. I was so lost in my grief I had spoken to no one since Rajila had died. He found me on my balcony and offered me a cup of tea. He placed two more cups on the table where our sisters would have sat, to honor and remember the two seats that would forever remain empty. We sat together, staring out at the forest but saying nothing.

He understood, just as I did, that words were inadequate in the face of such terrible loss. However, the presence of a friend who understood and shared my sadness was comforting. Days turned into weeks and slowly, we began to laugh again, he and I. Remembering times that were gone while making new memories as well.

It has been several months since I saw my friend. He is

the only reason I am looking forward to my visit to Fire Clan lands—aside from these humans I heard he has found.

A new species we have never encountered before crashed within his territory. The Fire Clan has taken them all in. Varus reports they are planning construction in their capital city to allow the wingless humans more freedom of travel, so they do not have to rely on our people. He claims they pride themselves on their independence.

Prince Varus has even mated a human, and she is already carrying his fledgling. He claims she is his linaya—his fated one. I am interested to learn more about these humans. They are the only species we've encountered that is biologically compatible, despite their many physiological differences, including the lack of any natural defenses.

Varus worries the other Clans will resent his people for harboring all the human females. He knows he need not worry about mine, however. For reasons we do not understand, more Earth Clan females survived the plague than those in other Clans.

Some believe we are favored by the gods for refusing to take part in conflicts between the other Clans. My people have remained neutral for thousands of cycles.

There are also rumors far and wide that our genes give us an advantage in fighting illness. Surviving females from other Clans have approached my Clan about mating with our males as a result. Clans usually do not interbreed, but I suppose the decline in our population has forced us to change our practices.

The females who have expressed interest in bonding with me do so not only for my genes but also for my status as Prince of the Earth Clan. I met one a few weeks ago who spoke of nothing but her desire to become my mate and Princess to our Clan.

I sigh and take another sip of my tea. That meeting left

me with heavy hearts. I want a mate who is my equal, who wants me for me instead of what I can offer her. If only the gods would grace me with a linaya, I could put an end to this search.

"Kaj." The sound of my mother's voice draws my attention to the doorway.

"Yes, Mother?"

"I wanted to speak with you before you leave tomorrow."

Now my curiosity is piqued. It's not as if I would have left without saying goodbye. For her to seek me out now—the night before I'm to depart—means it must be something important.

I motion for her to join me on the balcony. She sits across from me.

Her warm golden eyes stare across at me, and I think on how Father loves to tell the story of how excited she was when I was born. She was thrilled that my eyes were the same shade as hers and my scales were a deep forest green like his. My sister was the same—we were a perfect blending of our parents. "I wanted to discuss the issue of a potential mate bond, my son."

Sighing heavily, I turn my gaze out to the forest and take another drink of my tea. "Must we talk about this now?"

She places a hand on my forearm. "Yes, Kaj, we must. You are of an age that this should have already been decided. Hymila's father approached us with an offer."

My head jerks toward her. "Hymila? No. She only wants me for my title."

Mother purses her lips. "You do not know that, Kaj."

"Yes, I do," I protest. "She said as much last time we talked... when *she* offered herself to become my mate. I refused and my refusal still stands."

Father steps onto the balcony and it's obvious he's heard

us from the disapproving look on his face. "You are the heir. You must choose a mate."

A thought suddenly occurs to me and I narrow my eyes at them. "We've already had this conversation. Why are you bringing this up again the night before I am to leave?"

Mother's eyes dart to Father's and they exchange a knowing look.

It is as I suspected: A coordinated attack.

Crossing my arms, I sit back in my chair and then wait for whatever it is they have so carefully planned.

Mother takes my hand. "We spoke with Varus's parents. His mother and father are thrilled with his human mate, Lilly. They say she is the most enchanting creature they have ever seen."

"And there are several unmated human females in their group," Father adds.

I frown in confusion. "Are you saying that you want me to bond with a human?"

Mother nods encouragingly. "Varus and Lilly have the fated bond between them. Proof that the humans are blessings from the gods themselves. She is already carrying their fledgling."

Ah. So that is what this is about. My mother suspects that if one human female is fertile enough to become pregnant in less than a cycle with her mate, then the others must be as well. It is no secret she and my father long for grandchildren.

I must admit that I have wanted to meet the humans ever since I found out about Varus's mate, hoping that perhaps one may be fated to me as well. But I have tried to temper my hope so that I am not disappointed if it does not happen.

It is every Drakarian's dream to find their fated one, but it does not happen for all of us.

My parents exchange another glance and then look back at me, their expressions hopeful. After a moment, my mother speaks. "Will you at least consider the possibility of bonding to a human?"

Little do they know that I have been eagerly anticipating meeting the humans with the hope that one of them is fated to me. That my mark will appear the moment I see one of them and I will know, without doubt, that she is mine and I am hers. I had worried, however, that my parents might be upset if this occurred, especially since I've heard that the humans are practically defenseless compared to our people.

They lack claws, fangs, scales and even wings. All the basic things one should have to defend one's self against enemies or predators. From the way they have been described to me, I wonder how they have managed to survive as a species. But Varus goes on and on about his mate and how wonderful she is, insisting that she is strong in other ways.

A smile quirks my lips as I decide to tease my parents. "I have decided to lead a celibate life."

Father's eyes widen in shock and my mother gasps. "You cannot mean that," she says. "How could you even consider such a thing? You are heir to the Earth Clan throne and—"

I try but fail to suppress a grin and mother sighs in relief. So does Father.

He narrows his eyes but it is easy to see the amusement that dances behind them. "You nearly stopped both my hearts with your words, my son. I thought for a moment you were serious about celibacy."

I laugh. "I had to find a way to repay you for your coordinated attack."

Mother scoffs and then tips up her chin. "I do not know what you are talking about."

I cross my arms. "So you deny that this was a planned intervention before I left?"

Father grins as he looks to my mother. "Our son is wise. He knows us too well."

"Of course, he is wise," Mother smirks. "He takes after me."

She leans forward and takes both my hands, her golden eyes shining at me full of a mother's love. "While you are gone, your father and I will pray night and day to the gods for you to find your fated one among the humans as Varus has done. I long for you to be happy, Kaj."

A smile tugs at my lips. "And you also want many grand-children."

She laughs. "That too."

I sigh heavily. "I know you wish for me to find a mate. I wish for this as well. But I desire more than anything to have what the two of you do." I pause. "I pray to the gods that the mark on my chest will glow someday... that I will find my fated one and know, without doubt, that she was destined for me by the gods."

Father places a hand on my shoulder. "We wish this for you as well, my son."

One of the staff steps onto the balcony and then bows low before us. "Forgive my intrusion," he says. His gaze shifts to me. "Your cousin, Healer Ranas, is on the vid screen in the communication room. He says he must speak with you urgently, my prince."

Without hesitation, I rush to the communication room. As soon as I press the button on the vid screen, his face appears on the display. "Cousin, you must come quickly. We need help!"

"What is wrong?"

"The Wind Clan. They attacked the city and tried to steal the human females. We defeated them, but many are wounded. Can you send more Healers?"

I blink slowly, shocked. How could this have happened?

Females, regardless of species, are cherished and treasured among our people. Harming one goes against all codes of honor. "How many are injured?"

"About twenty humans."

Panic coils tightly in my chest. From what I've heard, their species does not heal as quickly as ours, even with the use of my Clan's healing fire. "We'll be there as soon as possible," I reply and then shut off the display.

I tap out a quick message to my parents, informing them that I am leaving immediately and assigning several more Healers to accompany me to the Fire Clan's lands. As soon as I'm done, I shift into my draka form and take to the sky. I had wanted to bid them goodbye, but there isn't time. Furiously pumping my wings, I ascend into the clouds.

Myriad thoughts flow through my mind. The last I'd heard, Prince Raidyn of the Wind Clan stole one of the human females from her crew in the desert. The only witness to this event was a human male named John, whom Varus does not trust.

Like myself, Varus does not believe Raidyn would have taken the female without good reason. Either she is his fated one or she was in danger. Either way, he would never harm her. However, the human male claims that Raidyn attacked them unprovoked and took the female against her will.

It does not make sense that the Wind Clan has now attacked and tried to take the humans from the Fire Clan capital. Why would they break their enduring treaty of non-aggression with Varus's people?

A bellow shakes the air behind me, and I'm relieved to find more Healers already following in my wake.

An Earth draka with copper scales comes up beside me and I immediately recognize Rowan—my personal guard. His light-green eyes meet mine, full of determination. "Allow me to accompany you, my prince."

I shake my head. "You do not have to come."

"I may not have trained as a Healer, but I can still blow healing fire. I wish to be of help."

It is no use arguing with him. Rowan is not just my personal guard, he is a close friend. Ever since we first learned of the humans, he has talked of nothing else. I know he comes as much to aid as he does to see the human females. Ever since word spread that Varus found his linaya among them, Rowan and almost all the other unmated males are hopeful they might find their fated ones among the humans, as well.

"Fine, but I do not know what we will find when we get there."

"What do you mean?"

"The humans are fragile creatures. I only hope we will reach them in time to be of use."

Rowan's face is a mask of grim determination as his pace quickens. "Let us hurry, then."

∼

As soon as we reach the city, my jaw drops. I take in all the destruction and ruin below. Several buildings have been razed to the ground. Piles of broken stone and rubble litter the streets.

I look to Rowan, whose eyes are wide as he, too, surveys the chaos beneath us. We make a long arc around the castle and land in a courtyard just outside the medical center.

I shift instantly and rush inside, bracing myself for what we might find. Rows of beds line the infirmary, many of them bearing what must be humans. Several cry out in pain, but it is the ones who lie still that concern me the most.

Any Healer knows that those patients who can voice their

discomfort are more likely to live, whereas those who have already gone quiet suffer from far worse injuries.

I spin to face my kin. "Quickly. Help any and all you can. I'm sure Healer Ranas is exhausted."

I scan the room and my suspicions are confirmed as soon as my gaze comes to rest upon my cousin. His eyes are glossed over with fatigue. I notice the healing fire he breathes on one of the injured humans is not as bright as it should be. I understand why he asked for help; healing so many has depleted his energy. Already, I can see his strength beginning to wane.

I start toward him, but a small hand on my forearm stops me in my tracks. I turn and look down to find a human female with long, brown hair. Her dark-green eyes stare up at me, reminding me of the lush forests that surround my home.

"Can you please help me sit up?" she asks in a small voice.

Dumbfounded, I nod. I brace one hand behind her upper back and she takes my other hand as I slowly pull her upright. I'm both shocked and disturbed by how small and slight she is compared to a Drakarian female. How does Varus keep from injuring his linaya while mating?

My eyes are drawn to her short, blunt nails. The texture of her golden skin is petal-soft, and her features are delicate. When she opens her mouth to speak again, I notice she has flat, white teeth instead of fangs. I heard her people did not have scales and lacked natural defenses, but my concerns have now doubled knowing their skin offers little protection against injury or the elements.

She grits her teeth in obvious pain as she bands one arm over her torso as if to brace herself.

"You should lie back down," I tell her. "You are injured."

Her gaze sweeps the room. "So is everyone else. I need help standing up, and then I should be fine."

I blink. Perhaps she is in shock. Why else would she be trying to stand while she is wounded?

"Wait," I whisper, hoping to calm her. "Allow me to heal you."

She shakes her head. "Ranas already did what he could."

Her casual use of only his name without a title suggests she knows him well. I'm about to ask for her name when she beats me to it.

"I'm Anna. I'm a doctor—Healer, I mean," she corrects herself. "I know Ranas is exhausted, so I want to do what I can to help."

"I am Kaj. I'm a Healer, as well. Ranas is my cousin," I explain. "I understand you wish to be useful, but you are injured and need to rest."

She lifts her determined gaze, extending one hand. "Please, help me stand. That's all I need."

My instincts want to argue that she should lie down, but the fire in her eyes tells me she will not listen even if I do.

"Allow me to assess your injuries, at least."

Reluctantly, she nods, disappointment evident in her features as she drops her hand. When she lifts her fabric coverings and bares her torso to me, I bite back a gasp. Dark, mottled discoloration covers almost her entire left side. If this is what her body looks like after Ranas has already treated it, I cannot imagine how badly she was originally injured. How did she survive such a devastating injury?

I meet her eyes, calm but insistent. "May I?"

"Sure. Anything to take away this pain."

I breathe my healing fire across her torso, watching in satisfaction as the bruising fades beneath the blue-green flame.

A soft sigh of contentment escapes her lips, and my hearts fill with happiness that I have brought her at least some measure of relief.

Despite her obvious pain, she gives me a smile that rivals the brightness of the sun. "Thank you. I feel so much better. Ranas couldn't do much for me since he had to conserve his energy, but he did heal the wound on my head. Thank you so much for taking care of the rest."

Panic constricts my chest when she mentions a head wound. The small bones of her form appear so delicate, I am concerned. "May I finish assessing your condition?"

She nods.

Parting the fine, long, silken brown hair on her head, I study her wound. It is healing, but not completely closed. It is as Ranas said; humans take longer than our kind to mend.

Ignoring her lingering pain, she grits her teeth and stands. For all I've heard of the weakness of humans, I would never suspect them as weak from the way this female acts. Her strength of will could rival even the strongest warriors of our kind. Her warm green eyes stare up at me, and when she smiles again, my hearts stop momentarily.

My nostrils flare as I draw in her distinct, delicate scent, reminiscent of the kalli flowers that grow near my home.

"We can probably get more done if we work as a team," she suggests, scanning my body. "What do you say?"

I marvel at her strength and determination. This female is amazing, and I am completely captivated. I give her an affirmatory nod and then puff out my chest, hoping to impress her.

It is a good plan. We can treat many more patients together than separately. "You begin and I will follow, treating whatever you cannot with my healing fire."

"All right, Kaj." She smiles. "Let's get this done."

I watch in wonder as she moves down the line of beds, tending to as many as she can. She may not possess healing fire like the members of my Clan, but she deftly uses tools and medicine instead to help the injured. I discreetly continue to observe her as I take care of my patients. She is as intelligent as she is beautiful, this female. Despite the severity of her injuries, I am impressed that she performs her job without complaint.

As if sensing my gaze upon her, she glances at me and sends a dazzling smile. I am completely enthralled with Anna.

A sharp noise of protest draws my attention and my gaze snaps to the bed beside me. A human female stares up at me with wide eyes full of terror. "Leave me alone! Go away!"

My brow furrows. "But I am here to help you."

"No!" she wails. "Leave us alone! All of you!"

Anna rushes to my side and takes the female's hand. "Enara, it's all right. They're here to help."

"No!" she protests. "They just want to hurt us like those other dragons tried to."

Anna places a hand on my forearm. "This is Kaj. He's a good guy. I promise. He helped me, too," she adds with a smile. "You can trust him."

I puff out my chest and tip my chin up with pride. It fills my hearts with joy knowing that I have already earned Anna's trust.

Meeting her bright green eyes, I find myself unable to speak, much less form a coherent thought. "Kaj, this is my friend, Enara. Enara, this is Kaj."

I bow low. "It is a pleasure to meet you, Enara."

"You, too." She gives me a quivering half-smile. "I'm sorry for the way I acted. I'm still a bit shaken up after... what happened."

I hate that the Wind Clan has caused these females to fear us. This is an entirely new world to them, and they are trying to start a life among our people. Their actions this day have caused the humans to doubt the intentions of all Drakarians.

It will take much time to repair the relationship between our two species.

"I understand," I reply gently, hoping to calm her. "But I vow that I will not harm you. I only wish to help."

As the female allows me to treat her, I cannot help but think on Varus's words. These humans have been through much and yet, they are resilient.

I glance down the long row of beds and notice Rakan—Varus's personal guard—leaning over one of the human females, his expression full of worry. I walk to his side.

Rakan lifts his gaze to mine. "She is still unconscious but stable. Ranas says she will be fine."

I place a hand on his shoulder. "This is good news."

"I failed her, Prince Kaj. I did not reach her in time." He clenches his jaw. "It is my fault Holly was hurt."

"From what I understand, you and the rest of the Fire Clan warriors are the reason the humans were saved and not taken. Surely, that is not a failure in her eyes."

It is easy to read in his expression that he cares deeply for this female. I wish I could offer him more comfort, but I cannot. I do not know if these females are like ours. A Drakarian female would never consider a male to be a worthy mate if he failed to protect her in any way. I only hope this human female forgives him.

I give him a parting nod and then glance over at Anna, observing as she treats another patient. She is brave, kind, intelligent and beautiful. Despite what I have heard about her people, they are stronger than they appear. And now that I've met Healer Anna, I long to know more about her.

CHAPTER 3

ANNA

K aj and I work side by side, making our way down each row of beds to tend the wounded.

Out of the corner of my eye, I study him. Tall, spiraling horns the color of jade decorate his head. Long green hair nearly the same shade as his scales falls around his shoulders. With golden eyes, a proud square jaw, and princely features, he's very handsome—for an alien dragon-man.

His arms and legs are thick and muscular. He's taller than any human I've ever met, and his shoulders are broad and strong. His abdomen and chest are layers of rippling muscle. His long, tapered tail swishes back and forth behind him as he tends to his patient. When I lift my gaze, I find him staring at me. His vertically slit pupils expand as if he likes what he sees, and his lips part in an irresistible smile. I could easily get lost in his golden eyes.

My heart flutters and my cheeks flush with warmth as I return his smile.

There's just something about him that draws me in. I dart another glance in his direction, admiring his confident posture. He leans down to ask Enara how she's feeling, and I notice he does his best to make her smile and laugh. He has an impressive bedside manner with his patients.

As if sensing my gaze upon him, he looks up at me and grins again before turning his attention to the next patient. I wonder if he's married—or as they say, mated. He doesn't have the glowing fate mark on his chest, but then again, not all mated Drakarians have found their linaya. Some marry simply for love like humans do.

I've heard the Earth Clan dragons are peaceful and have never taken sides in a war between Clans. The only member I met before Kaj was his cousin Ranas, but he never told me he came from a family of Healers.

Forcing myself to focus, I turn my attention to the next patient. The good news is every patient has stabilized now that more Healers have arrived from the Earth Clan to help. My side still aches, and my breath hitches whenever I turn too quickly, but I feel so much better since Kaj treated me. I'll have to thank him again later. Maybe we can talk a bit more, too. I find I'm curious about him.

My friend Talia was unconscious but recovering last time I checked on her. When I look down the row of beds, I notice she's awake and talking to Prince Llyr of the Water Clan. His blue scales are definitely not hard to miss. Even from here, it's easy to see how much he cares for her. He spends quite a bit of time with my friend and I wonder if feelings have developed between the two of them. If so, Talia hasn't mentioned anything to me.

A flash of light-gray scales catches my eye, and I freeze. My heart pounds as the Wind Clan dragon's ice-blue eyes meet mine. I only have a moment to panic before Skye emerges from behind him, taking his hand and dragging him toward me while beaming.

Although I'm stunned, I'm so happy to see her that I rush forward and hug her tightly. "Thank the Stars you're all right!" A stray tear escapes my lashes, but I quickly brush it away. "I've been so worried about you."

"I've missed you!" She pulls back and gestures to the Wind dragon beside her.

As I scan his face, I notice a long, jagged scar that starts just above his left brow and extends to the top of his cheek. I wonder how he avoided losing his eye to this injury. My jaw drops when I also notice the glowing pattern of the fate mark across his chest.

Eyes wide, I glance between him and Skye.

"Anna." She gestures to him. "This is my husband-slash-mate, Prince Raidyn of the Wind Clan."

"You're his fated mate?"

She nods and snuggles against him while he wraps a possessive arm around her shoulders.

I'm so floored, I don't know what to say. How can she just stand by his side like he never kidnapped her? All this time she's been gone, I've been worried sick. We all have.

"I don't understand. His people just attacked us, Skye, and I haven't forgotten that he stole you, too. How can you act like everything is fine?"

"He didn't steal me," she snaps defensively. "And the attack wasn't his fault."

I open my mouth to protest, but Raidyn cuts me off, his ice-blue eyes full of guilt.

"Forgive me," he says, bowing his head slightly as he covers his glowing mark with his free hand. "My cousin was the one responsible for what happened. He manipulated my father, the king, into condoning this attempt to steal away your people."

"It's all right now, though," Skye adds, positioning herself between us. "Raidyn banished his cousin, and his father is stepping down. We are going to make sure nothing like this ever happens again."

"*We?*" I ask incredulously.

"Yes," Raidyn confirms. "I will ascend the throne as king and Skye will be Queen of the Wind Clan."

I don't know how to respond. I want to believe that they're right—that their rule will prevent any further attacks—but I can't be sure. I remember how safe I felt this morning, but now all my false security has suddenly been ripped away. Even though Skye might be mated to the Wind Clan's king, I might never be able to trust their Clan after what happened today.

"Trust me, Anna," Skye takes my hand. "Raidyn is a good guy."

Her words strike a chord deep inside me. Aren't those the same words I used earlier to convince Enara to trust Kaj? I told her he was a good guy so she'd let him treat her. I suppose Skye is as right as I was; you can't judge an entire group of people based on the actions of a few.

Despite my lingering reservations, Skye is still my friend.

"Congratulations," I tell them, forcing a smile onto my face. I need to talk to her privately later to make sure that she is as happy as she seems and not just pretending to appease Raidyn.

I've spent enough time around Prince Varus and Lilly to know that he's a great guy who adores her. However, I've only just met Raidyn, and given what little I've witnessed of his people, I'm not entirely sure about his character yet.

Skye squeezes me in another quick hug before I move on to the next patient. "We'll talk later," she promises and heads to speak with Talia.

I'm only a few beds away when a deep, rumbling growl

fills the air. The hair rises on the back of my neck. I spin toward the sound and find Raidyn leveling a dark glare at John.

"You!" King Raidyn bites out. "You hurt my linaya. You tried to force-mate her."

John's eyes fly wide and he goes completely pale. He turns to run but trips over his own feet and falls backward. As soon as he hits the ground, he starts crawling away as fast as he can. "Wait! I can explain!" he cries. "Please don't kill me!"

Raidyn rushes toward him at supernatural speed. He hauls John off the floor, suspending him in the air by his collar as he bares his sharp, deadly fangs.

"You should be dead. You will die for daring to harm my mate," he hisses. "My vow."

"Stop!" Varus commands, striding across the room. "What is the meaning of this?"

Skye steps between Raidyn and Varus. "John attacked me when we were alone together, searching for Lilly. If Raidyn hadn't come along, he might have—" Her breath catches.

Raidyn says what she can't. "He tried to force-mate her, Varus. I witnessed his crime with my own eyes. He deserves death."

John? A rapist? Oh, Stars. I knew his account of how Skye was taken sounded odd, but now the story makes sense.

"Set him down," Varus commands.

Reluctantly, Raidyn does, releasing his grip.

John crumples to the floor, trembling with fear as he stares up at Raidyn.

"Is this truth?" Varus shoots a lethal glare at John.

"I—I—" He stumbles over his words, scrambling to face Varus. "She wanted it." He points accusingly at Skye. "She's the one who came onto me!"

Skye's expression darkens dangerously while she stalks toward him. "I rejected you several times, but you wouldn't listen. How dare you try to lie about what you did! What would you have done after you'd raped me—killed me? Left me to die? You disgust me."

Varus and Raidyn snarl at him, baring their fangs.

Suddenly John pulls a blaster from his belt and thrusts it toward Skye, sneering, "Yeah, that's exactly what I would have done. And now, we can die together."

My heart stops as a bright flash erupts from the barrel and races toward my friend. Raidyn jumps in front of her, spreading his wings wide to shield her from the blast. I watch in horror as the beam rips his wing and continues undeterred. Talia jumps up and pushes Skye out of the way at the last moment. She takes a hit to her side and crumples to the floor.

The room erupts into a flurry of chaos. I rush to her side, the sick smell of burning flesh clogging my nose. I stare in horror at the angry burn on her torso.

Prince Llyr hovers over her, panic marring his normally stoic face. "Talia!" he cries. "We need the Healer!"

"I'm here," I tell him, but his face tells me he was hoping for someone else—one of the Earth Clan Healers. I may not have the ability to breathe healing fire, but I'm not entirely useless. I press my hands to her wound as Healer Ranas rushes up beside me and Kaj hurries to help Raidyn.

A feral roar splits the air, and I turn to catch Raidyn lunging for John.

John raises the blaster to fire again, but Raidyn knocks it from his grasp and swipes out with his claws, slicing his throat wide open.

John's hands clamp over his neck. He opens his mouth, but only a choked gurgle escapes him. Crimson blood pours from the mortal wound, pooling around his body as the light fades from his eyes. One of the Healers rushes toward him, but I turn away to concentrate on Talia.

I'm a doctor—it's my job to heal indiscriminately—but I can't deny that I'm glad John is dead. He tried to rape Skye just like Edward tried to rape me. I'll never forget the look on his face when I blew him out of the airlock. Everyone believes Edward's death was an accident.

It's my darkest secret. I never told anyone about the murder. As a doctor, I always thought it would be impossible for me to ever even contemplate intentionally taking a life. But with Edward, I wish I'd killed him sooner. If I had, he wouldn't have been able to hurt anyone else.

Prince Llyr gathers Talia in his arms, frantically calling her name. I lift my hands from her wound so Ranas can run the scanner over her body.

"Place her back on the bed," he orders Llyr. "And remove that." He gestures to her robe.

Talia's brother Milo stands frozen in shock as we watch Prince Llyr extend his claws and tear the fabric away to expose her wound. Sticky blood pools below the side of her torso.

If I weren't so confident in Ranas's healing fire abilities, I'd be terrified. But I've seen what the blue-green healing flame of the Earth Clan can do, and I know he'll be able to heal her.

I am transfixed, watching her torn tissue knit together beneath Ranas's ministrations, but when his eyes meet mine, I recognize his fatigue. He stops and sends Llyr a sorrowful look. "I have used up most of my energy healing the others, so I am unable to mend this wound for now. But I promise you, my friend, she will live."

Llyr gapes at him. "You cannot leave her like this. She needs—" he starts, but Ranas raises a hand to silence him.

"I have already sent word to my Clan. A few of the Healers have already arrived and more are on the way. They should be entering the medical center shortly."

I scan the med center for Kaj and motion him over. He nods and I turn my attention back to my patient.

"She'll probably sleep for a few hours. It seems like the healing fire causes drowsiness in us humans." I face Llyr. "You're the one who saved her, right?"

He nods, and out of the corner of my eye, I notice Milo roll his eyes.

I give him a pointed look. After Skye's disappearance, he doesn't trust any of the Drakarians. I understand how he feels, but I also know that we have to be diplomatic if we want to survive here.

He frowns. "What? Why are you looking at me like that?"

"Prince Llyr saved your sister. The polite response would be to thank him, Milo."

"Thanks for saving Talia," he grumbles.

With a clenched jaw, Llyr lowers his gaze. "I am sorry for what the Wind Clan has done. It is not our way."

Milo scoffs. "Not your way?" He gestures animatedly toward the door. "I just witnessed an epic dragon battle that suggests otherwise."

He's right. As much as I hate to admit it, even *I'm* not sure we're as safe with these Drakarians as we thought. Despite all the kindness the Fire Clan has shown us, they are a lethal race of warriors. Since we're biologically capable of carrying their children, I worry that those who are desperate for a mate could be willing to do anything to obtain one— including using force.

Llyr faces Talia's brother. "I promise you that we will do everything in our power to make sure no such crime is committed again."

Milo crosses his arms over his chest and sits back, leveling a glare at Llyr. "We'll see about that."

Varus approaches us with Raidyn at his side, his torn wing already healed.

Kaj trails them. I smile up at him, thankful he is here. I turn and then gently squeeze Talia's hand. "Healer Kaj is here, and he's going to take care of you, all right? I'll be back to check on you shortly."

Her eyes are still closed, but I know she's heard me when she squeezes my hand in return.

"Do not worry," Kaj adds. "I have enough energy to heal your friend."

"Thank you. I appreciate all your help."

He bows his head. "There is no need to thank me. After all you have suffered, I am honored that you work alongside me and entrust the care of your people to me even though we have broken your trust this day."

"I won't lie—the attack scared me. But I know that I can't judge every Drakarian by the actions of a few people."

His golden eyes hold mine for a moment before he dips his chin in subtle acknowledgment and returns his attention to Talia.

Although I've only just met him, something about Kaj makes me trust him. Trust has never come easily for me, especially with men, after what Edward did to me. However, Kaj somehow makes me feel safe.

He makes me feel other things too. Things that I don't want to focus on right now because they will probably only lead to trouble. I sigh heavily as I think back on his golden eyes and the way he looked at me earlier. He's handsome, intelligent and kind. There's something about him that makes me want to know more.

Shaking my head, I push the errant thoughts from my mind and move on to the next patient, forcing myself to focus on my work.

I go to check on my roommate—Holly. Her eyes are closed. Her normally long golden hair is streaked red with blood. She had a head wound, but Ranas's healing fire stopped the bleeding. Rakan—Varus's personal guard—sits in a chair beside her bed.

I look to him. "Has she been awake at all yet?"

His crimson eyes snap up to mine, full of panic. "Is it a bad sign that she is still unconscious?"

My poorly phrased question has made him worry and that was not my intent. He cares for Holly. That much has been clear from the moment his people first found us in the desert. But I don't know if she returns his affections. "No, I was just curious," I reassure him.

I run my med scanner over her form and study the readings. "According to this, she's doing well. Her body is healing."

His shoulders sag forward a bit in relief and he dips his chin in a subtle nod. "Thank you, Healer Anna."

Rakan is a good guy. I'm glad Holly has someone like him watching over her while she's unconscious. I've always thought that patients do better when they have someone with them while they're recovering.

I sigh heavily when I catch myself darting another glance at Kaj. He seems like a good guy as well. But, I can't afford to be distracted right now.

I'm still trying to find my place in this new world. There's so much left to learn if I want to practice medicine here.

CHAPTER 4

KAJ

I study Anna's retreating form, marveling at how calmly and efficiently she goes about her work. Several of the humans are visibly distraught to the point of tears after witnessing John's death, but not Anna. No, my female is strong. She simply moves on to the next patient, helping as much as she can. For one who lacks healing fire, she excels at her work.

I finish healing her friend, Talia, as quickly as I can. Prince Llyr seemed especially protective of her, but I did not find the fate mark upon his chest. I wonder if he recognizes Talia as his regardless. I know that the mark does not always appear instantly.

Llyr is my friend, so I decide that I will ask him. I am curious to know if he senses a connection to this human. I think I feel a connection to Anna, but I am uncertain. I've discreetly glanced at my chest several times since I met her, wondering if my fate mark would appear while we were speaking, but it did not. Perhaps I am merely attracted to her, though my instincts tell me I feel something more. I am eager to consult Llyr because I suspect he and I are experiencing the same thing.

A glimmer of light catches my eye. I look down and my jaw drops when the fate mark coalesces across my scales, glowing directly between my hearts.

I still as the realization hits me. I was right—I *have* found my fated one. My gaze immediately finds Anna across the room. It is her. It must be. I know in my hearts that she is mine.

Though I'm desperate to speak to her, my duty compels me to make sure all the humans are tended to first. Talia lifts her blue eyes to mine as I breathe my healing fire across her wound. I find myself longing to stare into the green eyes of my mate, instead.

I do all that I can, but humans take much longer to heal than our people. When I explain this to Llyr, he does not understand. Now, he's angry at me, accusing me of not tending to her properly. I suspect his aggression has something to do with his feelings toward this female. He is acting like a male who has found his fated one.

I open my mouth to explain this to him again, but Talia interrupts first. "Llyr, stop."

His gaze returns to her and his expression immediately softens. His actions are definitely those of a male hovering over his mate. I search his chest again for the fate mark but still find none.

"I'm fine, Llyr," she says. "I swear."

"But you are still hurting. You should not be in pain."

She lifts and drops her shoulders. "It's not that bad. I feel much better than I did earlier." She swings her legs off the bed. "In fact, I think I'd like to take a walk. Stretch my muscles a bit."

I stare down at her, surprised. Though she is injured, just

like my mate, she is already getting up. "You should rest," I insist, not wanting to be on the receiving end of Llyr's wrath. Even now, he glares at me as if I were somehow to blame for her stubbornness.

She rolls her eyes. "Look, I know you think all humans are pitiful weaklings, but we're not that fragile. I'd like to move around a bit, get my blood flowing again."

These humans have a strong will, like female Drakarians. I find myself impressed by their strength in the face of all they went through this terrible day. Although I believe Talia should rest, I've observed enough of human females in only half a day to understand that they are as fierce as they are stubborn.

"Fine," I tell her as I dart a glance at Llyr. "But someone should escort you, just in case."

Llyr's eyes drop to my chest. His mouth drifts open when he spots the fate mark pattern glowing on my scales.

His gaze snaps up to mine. "Who is it?"

I scan the room for Anna but do not see her. Closing my eyes, I draw in a deep breath. Her distinct and delicate scent lingers close by. Already, my body is becoming attuned to hers. "She is near. I can sense it."

Drawn to seek out my mate, I leave Prince Llyr to his human and follow the scent of mine into the castle. I find her seated on one of the carved k'lor benches in the palace garden. "How are you feeling?"

She sends me a tired smile. "Exhausted. How about you?" She rubs at her shoulder. "My muscles are so tense I feel like they're going to snap."

Panic stops my hearts. "That can happen to your body? Please, allow me to tend to you before your muscles snap."

She laughs. "No! I wasn't speaking literally. I'm fine. My muscles are just a little sore from overuse."

"Why did you not say something earlier?" I gently chastise

her. "You shouldn't have worked so hard this day. In fact, you should not have been working at all. You were still recovering when you insisted upon getting out of bed."

She shakes her head. "I'm fine. It's not a big deal, all right?"

I eye her carefully, unsure if I should believe her. I do not like the way she dismisses her health so easily. I can see that I must take great care to ensure she does not overwork herself. "Perhaps more of my healing fire will help. If you will allow me, I will tend to you."

A pink bloom spreads across her cheeks while she nods. I sit beside her and dip my hand beneath the neckline of her robe, sliding the fabric back to expose her shoulders. Her skin is soft beneath my fingers, and as my gaze travels down her chest, I notice the gently rounded mounds of her ample breasts peeking above the fabric. Drakarian female's chests are flat; they do not have breasts like these. I wonder if they are as soft as the rest of her skin. My fingers ache to trace every *tarem* of her body.

Drawing in a deep breath, I mentally chastise myself for my errant thoughts. She needs healing, and I will care for her.

She presents her back to me, and I brace myself on the bench behind her. I gather the long strands of her lovely brown hair in my hand, marveling at the silken texture, and pull it over her shoulder to expose her back. Gently, I exhale the blue-green healing flame across her shoulders and neck. She releases a deep sigh of contentment and leans into me. I struggle to suppress the low growl of arousal that vibrates deep in my chest at the enticing sound but manage to contain it.

The last thing I want is to place my needs above hers. I am desperate to speak to her about our connection, but that conversation must wait until she is completely healed. Right now, relieving her pain and taking care of her is my greatest priority.

When I am finished, I begin to massage her shoulders and neck. "Your scales," she says as she relaxes against me, "are as smooth as silk."

"You like them?" I ask, even as the scent of her need blossoms in the air around us, already providing me with an answer.

"*Mmmhmmm*," she hums softly as she allows her head to fall back and rest on my chest.

Suddenly, her head jerks up, and she spins to face me. Nervously, she reaches up and tucks a stray tendril of hair behind her ear. "Sorry, I—I didn't mean to get too comfortable there. I—" Her gaze drops to my chest, and her eyes widen as she stares at the fate mark swirling across my scales. "You didn't have that earlier."

I am thrilled that she has finally noticed. Now that she has brought it up, I can explain everything to her. "You are my linaya—my fated one. You need not apologize. It is no burden to care for you, my beautiful mate."

Her lovely pink lips part beneath my gaze. I saw Raidyn's human mate put her mouth on his earlier, and I wonder if my mate will wish to do so with me. The humans call it kissing. Even though my people do not share this custom, as I study her mouth, I find myself eager to try.

But that will have to wait. Although Anna is probably as eager as I am to seal our bond, I will insist that she recover first. "I will ask Varus to prepare us a room so that you may rest. I will care for you while you are healing. And I believe it would be wise to delay our first mating until after you are fully recovered."

She blinks. "First... mating?"

Her expression makes me wonder if she does not understand what I mean. She is a healer, so surely, she understands the concept of joining one's body to a mate. However, perhaps her species is sheltered and does not discuss such things. A few races on the Galactic Federation Council are this way.

I do not wish to embarrass her, so I take her hand gently as I stare deeply into her lovely green eyes. "Yes. A first mating is when a bonded pair decides to join their bodies as one. It is a beautiful experience, from what I have heard, and—"

She scoffs and pushes me away. "I know what mating is," she growls. "But why do you just assume you're going to mate with *me?*"

I glance at the glow on my chest, then lift my gaze back to her, arching a brow. "Because you are my fated one. My linaya." I point to the mark for emphasis. "This tells me that you are mine and that we will mate only each other. If the gods bless us, we will make many fledglings together."

Her jaw drops as a strange, deep-crimson coloring flares across her cheeks and the bridge of her nose. From my studies, I understand that many creatures change colors to indicate they are excited, aroused, or nervous. I do not know what she feels, though I myself am experiencing a strange combination of all three at the moment.

Never did I believe I could be so blessed as to find my linaya. For the gods to have chosen one as intelligent and beautiful as Anna is more than I could have ever hoped for. It is my deepest wish that she finds me attractive as well. I will do anything to please my mate.

"But I—I don't even know you." She stumbles over her words. "How can you want to mate someone you don't know?"

I freeze for a moment, then frown. Perhaps the injury she sustained to the back of her head has affected her memory. "I *do* know you. Do you not remember? We met a few hours ago," I explain slowly. "I am Kaj of the Earth Clan, and you told me that you are Anna. You are a human from Earth, and I am Drakarian. We are in the Fire Clan territory and have just fought off an attack. You told me that you had suffered a head injury, so I wish to assess it because I fear it may be affecting your memory."

I move toward her to part her hair again and check on the wound at the back of her skull.

She jerks away. "I'm not having memory issues," she hisses indignantly.

I cock my head to the side. "But you said that you did not know me, when clearly, we have met before."

She huffs and rolls her eyes in that curious gesture again —which Varus explained as one of frustration or annoyance. "What I mean is, I only just met you today. I'm not going to mate with you, Kaj."

"Of course not," I reply incredulously. Does she think I am a selfish male who thinks only of his own needs? Yes, my stav is hard and pressing insistently against the inside of my mating pouch with want to mount my beautiful mate and claim her as mine. But I hold it back because she is not completely healed of her injuries. "I would never pressure you into a first mating. We will wait until you are fully recovered."

Her jaw drops again, and she stares up at me with a look that borders on disbelief. She shoots to her feet, and I do the same, ready to assist her to a bed so that she may lie down and rest.

I move closer, but she puts a hand on my chest and tips up her chin. "I'm not yours. I belong to nobody but myself. Got it?"

CHAPTER 5

ANNA

His brows draw together. "I do not understand. Are you saying you do not wish to be my mate?"

"I don't know you."

His eyes flash with worry. "Please. Allow me to assess the wound on your head. I am concerned that—"

He reaches for me, but I bat his hand away. "There's nothing wrong with my head *or* my memory," I snap. "We only just met. I'm not going to marry you after half a day."

Understanding dawns on his face. "Ah, I believe I understand."

I sigh in relief. "You do. Oh, thank the Stars. I thought—"

"You wish to spend more time together before we mate. You want to appraise me. Make certain that I will be a good mate to you." He nods firmly. "Do not worry, Anna. We may make use of the mating chase, in our own way. Perhaps, I shall chase you on foot to prove my worthiness to you when you are ready."

I open my mouth to protest that that wasn't what I meant,

but I quickly snap my jaw shut when he steps back and tilts up his chin, puffing out his chest.

I've heard rumors of the mating chase. Lilly told me that a Drakarian man chases his mate, demanding she give herself to him. If he catches her, she has a choice. If she refuses him, they part ways. If she accepts, they claim one another right then and there.

He then leans forward slightly, flexing one very impressive bicep toward me. "I am strong. I will protect you and our future fledglings with my life." He inches closer and bows to my height. "You may now ask me anything you'd like to assess my worth. The mating chase can wait until after you are fully healed."

There have not been many times in my life when I've been rendered speechless, but this is definitely one of them.

I take a moment before I reply. "Look, you're a nice guy and all, but... it's been a long day and this"—I gesture to him —"is all a bit more than I anticipated. I'm tired and I need to go lie down for a bit."

He nods. "Of course. You are still healing. I will ask Varus to prepare our chambers so that I may care for you."

"No," I tell him firmly. As friendly as he seems, I don't want to leave any room for mixed signals here. I already made that mistake with Edward, and I promised myself I'd never slip up again. "You don't understand. I *do not* want to share a room with you."

He stares blankly as if he can't believe what I've just said. "But the fate mark." He points at his chest. "You are mine and I am yours."

"No, I am not. I don't belong to anyone. Now, leave me alone."

"You wish for me to leave your side?" he asks incredulously.

I don't waver for a second. "Yes."

"But I—"

"What's going on here?" Lilly calls.

I turn to face her, gesturing exasperatedly. "Kaj insists that I'm his. I've told him that I don't belong to anyone and—"

"The fate mark." Varus gasps, his eyes glued to Kaj's chest. "Anna is your linaya?"

"Yes," Kaj replies.

"No, I'm not," I huff, crossing my arms. "Just because he calls me that doesn't mean I am."

"But you are." Varus's tone is solemn. "The gods have willed it. Whether you choose to accept it or not is entirely up to you, however."

I notice that he sends Kaj a pointed look at his last sentence.

I turn to Lilly for help. She shakes her head softly, turning to her mate. "Can you give us a moment?"

He nods and puts a hand on Kaj's shoulder to guide him away.

I turn back to her. "Is this how it happened with you and Varus?"

"Not exactly. But I think we should probably include Skye in this conversation."

Reluctantly, I nod.

CHAPTER 6

KAJ

Although I am hesitant to leave my mate, I follow my friend Varus farther into the palace gardens. He looks to one of his guards. "Find Raidyn. Ask him to join us here."

The guard nods and then walks away.

Varus and I take a seat on one of the long benches surrounding a fire pit. I have always enjoyed this part of the palace. The lush greenery and vibrant flowers remind me a bit of my home. It is strange that a garden such as this can exist in a desert, but Varus has explained that there are many natural underground springs from which he and his people draw water.

I wonder if Anna enjoys these gardens as well. If so, I believe she would be pleased to live in the Earth Clan territory. But when I think on how she reacted only a moment ago to my glowing fate mark, I doubt she'll ever wish to visit my home.

Raidyn joins us only a few moments later. He frowns at

Varus. "I received your message and—" He stops speaking abruptly when he sees my chest. A wide grin splits his face. "Congratulations, my friend. You have found a mate as well? Who is the fortunate female?"

I open my mouth to speak, but Varus beats me to it. "She is one of the humans, named Anna. She is a healer among their people and a good friend to both our mates."

"She is not pleased with me," I add soberly. "The way she refused me... I suspect she wishes she were paired with a different male."

Varus pats my shoulder. "Do not worry, my friend. Human females are different. They do not feel the pull of the bond as we do. They must be courted first."

Crossing his arms over his chest, Raidyn nods. "You must convince them that the fate bond is truth, for they do not experience it as we do."

Varus purses his lips. "But do not take any advice from Raidyn."

"Why not?" I frown. "He seems to be happily mated."

Varus sighs heavily. "Because stealing your mate away to convince her that she is yours is not a good plan."

My eyes snap to Raidyn. "So it *is* truth? You stole your mate?" I ask incredulously.

He scowls. "I did not *steal* her. I *rescued* her," he corrects. "To shield her from the wrath of my father, I took her to my family's estate."

I'm eager to hear more. "And then?"

He tips his chin up with pride. "At first, she did not desire me. But after a few days alone, I was able to convince her that I was a worthy mate."

"So, if I take Anna somewhere private, you believe she might change her mind about me? Decide that she wishes to become mine?"

Raidyn nods while Varus stares at us both, aghast.

"You cannot steal a female away from her people just to convince her to be yours," he exclaims, throwing his hands in the air.

"I won't steal her," I counter. "I will ask her to come to my territory… spend some time with me there."

He frowns and then crosses his arms over his chest. "And what if she does not wish to go?"

"I… do not know." My shoulders sag in defeat. "I only know I am worried that she will reject me. That she'll find me lacking in some way. It concerns me that she did not show even the slightest of interest in the mating chase when I mentioned it. That cannot be a good sign."

Varus places a hand on my shoulder. "The mating chase is not something her people normally do. Human females must be courted. Only then will she know if she desires you."

"How do I court her?" I ask, my tone slipping into desperation.

"Spend time with her. Get to know her better."

I nod, understanding. "I will do this." I glance between the two of them. "It is odd that humans do not have fate bonds naturally, is it not?"

Varus and Raidyn share a knowing glance before Varus steps forward. "There are a few… other things you should know about humans."

"Like what?"

Raidyn turns to me, a sly smirk on his lips. "If she accepts you, there is a spot on a human female's body that gives great pleasure if stimulated during mating."

My mind replays images of Anna's soft, pink lips and luminous green eyes. "Please, share all you know of human courtship and mating rituals. I wish only to please my mate."

CHAPTER 7

ANNA

Lilly leads us to the private rooms she shares with her mate, Prince Varus. As we cross the bedroom, I notice the covers on the bed are rumpled. She has told me they make love at least twice a day. It's no wonder she got pregnant so quickly.

She leads us onto her balcony, and I gasp at the beautiful view. Light glows mesmerizingly from the city below. Amid the dim lighting, the only evidence of the day's attack is the dark spot not far from the castle where the human apartments stood. I remember how safe and at peace with our new life I felt just this morning. Now... I just don't know.

So much has changed in such a short amount of time. Who knew that by the end of the day, a Drakarian would declare that I'm supposed to be his?

We sit around a small table and I marvel at the several pots that line the balcony, overflowing with beautiful glowing blue flowers. Their vines climb up the walls of the castle, framing the entrance back into the bedroom. Despite that we're in a desert, I'm reminded that it's still beautiful here.

It makes me wonder about the other territories. There is still so much of this world we haven't seen. I think of how Varus tried describing them to us only a few nights ago and my thoughts turn to Kaj. Varus said the Earth territories are made up of mountains with dense forests and thick jungles.

One of the servants pours us some tea. Tea is apparently the drink of choice for Drakarians. The blend they drink has a bitter aftertaste, but it's not entirely bad. I'm already getting used to the taste. Besides, Varus swears up and down that his tea has immune-enhancing properties even for humans, and Ranas confirmed this when I asked him.

The Fire Clan people have been kind, helping us get settled and all. But I don't know about the other Clans. Raidyn may be Skye's mate now, but I'm worried about her living with the Wind Clan after they attacked the city.

Her expression is dreamy as she tells me all about the time she spent with Raidyn at his family's secluded estate. On a floating island, no less. Granted, they were hiding out from his father who wanted to imprison her because he thought humans were dangerous, but I'm still impressed.

When she finishes her story, I lean forward. "So... he didn't really steal you like we thought he did?"

She shakes her head. "No. He saved me from John."

I'm still having a hard time wrapping my mind around the fact that John tried to rape her. Raidyn killed him, and I'm glad. He would have raped Skye if Raidyn hadn't stopped him. It seems that Raidyn wasn't the villain, after all. It's comforting to know that rape is considered a crime on this world, yet I wonder about the Wind Clan's motives for trying to steal us if they did not plan to mate with us.

"What did Raidyn's people plan to do with us?"

She sighs. "They think that because Raidyn and Varus

have found human linayas, perhaps other Wind Clan warriors would find theirs, as well. They thought Varus was sequestering all the women away from the rest of the Clans so that they wouldn't even have a chance to see us, let alone find out if they might be fated to one of us."

"They weren't planning to rape us, then? Force us into bonding with their men?"

"No!" She shakes her head emphatically, as does Lilly. "They would never."

Despite their vehement denial, I'm not so sure.

"Varus is good friends with Prince Kaj," Lilly says, changing the subject. "He's told me a lot about him."

My mouth drifts open. "He's a prince?"

"He didn't tell you?"

"I, uh... it didn't come up."

"Hey!" Talia's cheerful voice draws my attention.

She walks over to us as I look her up and down. "You're feeling better?"

She grins. "Yeah, Prince Kaj took care of me."

My expression falls. "Does everyone know he's a prince except for me?"

Her brow furrows. "What are you talking about?"

"Kaj's chest started glowing with the fate mark for Anna," Skye explains.

Talia's jaw drops. "Oh my gosh. Congratulations!" I don't understand why she's smiling from ear to ear until she adds, "I wish Llyr's fate mark would appear for me."

"You like Llyr?" Lilly asks. "Have you told him?"

She shakes her head.

"Why not?" Skye asks.

She lowers her gaze to her hands. "What good would it do? I mean, what if his fate mark appears for someone else? I don't want to risk my heart only to lose him later. He swears he can feel in his hearts that we're meant to be, but without the mark, how can he be so sure?"

Lilly takes her hands. "Varus said the fate mark can take a while to appear, even if a Drakarian already recognizes his linaya."

A tear slips down her cheek. "But who knows if that's true when bonding a human? I mean, we're two different species, Lilly. Besides," she turns to Skye, "both of your mates had the mark right away, didn't they?"

They both nod. She turns to me, her eyes bright with tears. "You're so lucky, Anna. Kaj already displays the mark, so you know for sure you're supposed to be together."

I lower my gaze, both pitying and envying my friend. If Llyr's chest glowed with the fate mark for her, she would be with him in an instant. But my feelings are more complicated. I wish I could trust, but after what Edward did to me, I've feared getting too close to anyone.

"So, what are you going to do about Kaj?"

I shrug. "I... I don't know. I mean, I only just met him today."

Lilly takes my hand. Her eyes meet mine. "He's not like Edward, Anna." My friend knows me so well. Lilly, Talia, and Skye are the only ones who know that Edward tried to rape me. "If he were, Varus would not be his friend. Why don't you try to get to know him and see if you have anything in common? I mean... did you feel anything when you first met him? I saw you two talking for a while."

My cheeks flush with warmth at the memory of meeting him. There's no denying Kaj is handsome. I did feel an instant attraction to him, but that's not the same as love at first sight. "He's my type, if that's what you're asking. Or at least he seems to be, from what little I know. Things were going well—we were just getting to know each other—when he sprung the whole *you're-my-mate* speech on me this evening and ruined everything."

"Well then," Skye smiles brightly. "That's a good start, don't you think?"

I force a smile onto my face, hoping they'll stop trying to convince me. I certainly hope it's a good start because I don't want to think about what could happen if I upset Kaj.

What I don't tell my friends is that deep down, I'm terrified. I'm worried this nice guy routine is all just an act like it was for Edward. I'm afraid we'll get close, close enough that I'll let down my guard and then...

I shudder inwardly.

It's late by the time I finally return to my new room in the palace. A large four poster bed made of dark wood floats in the center of the room. The thick red comforter looks plush and inviting. In the corner is a small fireplace and despite its size it puts out quite a bit of heat.

Varus said the Drakarians have never used their fireplaces as much as they have since we arrived. Apparently, they are able to regulate their body temperatures more effectively than humans.

A light breeze blows in from the balcony, swaying the silken red curtains back and forth. If it wasn't so cold in the desert at night I'd be tempted to leave the door open. But I know it will only get cooler, so I move to close the door.

After I take a bath in the sunken bathing pool of the cleansing room, I wrap myself up in a robe and lie down in bed. Staring up at the ceiling, I think about my conversation with my friends. Lilly and Skye seem content with their mates. Poor Talia lamented how she wished Llyr's chest would glow with the fate mark for her.

I know she must think I'm ungrateful, but it's different for me and Kaj. I only just met him, whereas she at least has spent more than half a day getting to know Llyr.

With a heavy sigh, I roll over onto my side. Maybe if the Wind Clan hadn't attacked us today, I'd feel differently. But Drakarians are possessive, and even without the fate bond, the Wind Clan was willing to steal us just because we are female and they want a chance at finding their fated mates.

Part of me wonders if Kaj won't take no for an answer. That's what concerns me.

I draw in a deep breath and force the terrible memories of Edward from my thoughts. I don't want to live my life in fear, but that's easier said than done. I wish Kaj was just a regular guy that I could date, instead of my supposed fated mate. I know how important the fate bond is to the Drakarians.

I wonder how long he'll be patient with me before he decides he has waited long enough.

CHAPTER 8

KAJ

Although I am certain the humans still recovering in the medical center are well cared for, I go to check on them anyway. Ranas is still there when I enter. His eyes dart to the fate mark on my chest.

He claps a hand on my shoulder. "I have heard you are to bond with Anna." He grins. "She is a good match for you, I think. She is brilliant, and her personality suits yours—thoughtful and introspective like you."

I nod. "In only the short time I have spent in her presence, I have been amazed by how quickly she seems to be adapting to our world. Even without our healing fires, she is a capable healer in her own right." I look down at my hands. "But she does not want me as her mate."

Ranas shakes his head. "The humans are different, cousin. They neither recognize nor feel the pull of the bond. Give her time to get to know you." He places a hand on my shoulder and meets my eyes evenly. "But whatever you do, you must not pressure her. There is… something you must know about Anna."

The look on his face worries me. "What is wrong, Ranas? Tell me."

"I have spent much time with Anna, teaching her to use our technology. She is comfortable with me now, I believe. But at first, she was wary of my presence. I asked Princess Lilliana about Anna because they are good friends, and she told me that something happened to Anna on the ships. Something that made her cautious of males."

My chest tightens. "Someone hurt my mate?"

Frowning, he nods. "That is the impression I received. However, I do not know the details, for she would share no more with me."

My hands curl into fists at my side at the thought of someone abusing my mate. My opinion of human males is dropping with each passing moment. A growl rumbles my chest. "The human males should be kept isolated in the palace at all times until we know they can be trusted not to harm the females."

Ranas shakes his head. "The same could be said for us, after the attack by the Wind Clan this day."

His words fill me with shame, for they are truth. Perhaps that is why Anna is so unwilling to accept that we are fated. If she already distrusts males because of past trauma, the events of this day will have only deepened that conviction. This may make it even harder to convince her to be mine.

As if reading my thoughts, Ranas places a hand on my shoulder. "Give her time to know you, cousin. Allow her to see that you are not a male who would ever harm a female."

Ranas speaks wisely; I cannot expect Anna to accept me outright when she has experienced something that has instilled fear in her hearts. I must be patient. I must prove to her that I am worthy to be her mate.

When I return to the palace gardens to chat with my friends, I'm surprised to find Prince Llyr has joined them.

Raidyn is addressing him. "They do not recognize the bond as we do. It was the same for Skye and me."

"And for Lilliana and me," Varus agrees. "Her species does not experience fate bonds naturally. You must be patient." He side-eyes Raidyn, who frowns. "Unlike this one."

"I *was* patient with my mate," Raidyn counters.

Varus snorts. "Then perhaps Skye was speaking of another male when she told Lilliana about your time together. She told my mate that you insisted she was yours from the first moment you met. That hardly counts as patience."

Raidyn's expression grows thunderous. "I did not force her to accept me, if that is what you are implying."

Varus snickers with a smirk. "No, I am merely stating that you wore her down with your insistence that she was your mate. And eventually, she accepted."

"I wooed her," he growls. "I did not *wear her down*."

Varus claps a hand on Raidyn's shoulder and gives him a good-natured grin. "Do not be angry with me, my friend. I am merely speaking truth."

Raidyn narrows his eyes, and Varus laughs again, louder this time.

There must be more to the story between Raidyn and his mate than what I gathered earlier. I thought their love developed naturally as they spent time alone together as he suggested, but it seems he was more proactive than I realized.

Varus sobers. "When do you leave?"

"As soon as possible," Raidyn replies. "After all the damage done by my family, I must make sure order is restored to my kingdom. I do not know if Skye will wish to come with me since the Wind Clan is in so much turmoil."

My mouth drifts open in shock. I do not know if I could be parted from Anna now that I've found her. However, I understand Raidyn's concerns. His kingdom may not be the safest place for his mate if there are any who disagree with the new transfer of power.

"If she chooses to stay behind, we will keep her safe," Varus assures him. "My vow."

Llyr steps forward. "With your kingdom in turmoil, you will need the support of the other Clans, will you not?"

"What are you suggesting?" Raidyn demands. "That I am unable to rule?"

"No," he denies. "I am merely stating that together, we are stronger. I'm certain you both remember the days long past when all the Clans gathered once every cycle to celebrate the peace between the four Clans. I wish that we could see those days again. Do you not?"

All of us nod in slow understanding.

His suggestion is sound. To ensure the safety of the humans, we must stop all the petty bickering between us. More importantly, peace between all Clans will help my mate to feel safe. I step into the circle. "I agree that would be a wise decision."

It has been many cycles since our Clans have come together to celebrate. That the four of us are all peacefully negotiating is a miracle in itself, considering all the infighting staining our past.

Only the Earth Clan has consistently stayed neutral. Perhaps it is because our healing fire abilities are not destructive, and we rarely use our flame and frostfire, unlike the other Clans.

I allow my gaze to drift over my friends before turning my attention back to Llyr. "If I remember correctly, the Water Clan was scheduled to host the next celebration before the practice ended cycles ago. Is that not correct?"

Llyr bows his head to me. "My Clan would be honored to host the revived gathering."

"Once there, we could discuss how best to acclimate the humans to our world," Varus adds.

Llyr's brows pinch together. "What do you mean?"

"At heart, the humans are explorers. They set out from their world on colony ships in search of a paradise planet."

"Which is what, exactly?" I ask, curious to know what the humans would consider an optimal environment.

Raidyn glances at Varus. "A place with plentiful water and vegetation."

I understand why he watched for Varus's reaction to his words. Although they are the first to take in the humans, it seems his lands are not exactly what they were hoping to find for their settlement. Though I sympathize with my friend, I agree with the humans. The desert landscape is harsh and unyielding. I have always imagined it must be difficult to live in such a dry, barren place.

"But each of our territories presents different challenges for a human," Raidyn continues. "The Fire territory is dry and lacking in vegetation. The Wind territory, despite its hospitable climate, is built on a series of floating islands. The Earth territory is mountainous, covered in thick jungle, and most of your dwellings are built into the sides of the mountains. The Water territory is mostly ocean, and during the winter, mostly ice. The humans are wingless—they cannot move about as freely as our kind can."

He is right, although I am reluctant to admit it. Despite the harsh environment, Varus's lands are more suited to wingless residents than the rest.

Llyr must realize this, too, because he turns to Varus. "Despite lacking the 'paradise' that the humans crave, your cities can easily be modified to accommodate their needs."

"The same could be done in my lands," I interject. The

very thought fills me with hope. I want my mate to be happy. Perhaps I can convince Anna to visit our territory while I court her.

Llyr's gaze drops to my chest, examining the dim glow of the fate mark on my scales. "Who has drawn your attention?"

I sigh heavily. "The healer, Anna."

"Has she accepted you?"

Clenching my jaw, I shake my head. I note that he runs his hand absently over his chest with a saddened air.

Cautiously, I ask, "Do you feel the pull of the bond as well?"

"Yes, I feel it toward Talia. But she refuses to accept me."

My head jerks back in surprise. "Why?"

"She is worried that I have mistaken her for my linaya because the fate mark has not appeared to confirm what I already know in my hearts. She does not want to fall in love with me and risk losing me to someone else."

At this moment, I feel as if we are two kindred spirits, each longing to be claimed by our mates. Except, if he had the mark, his mate would accept him, I think to myself bitterly.

I look to Varus. "Has Lilliana mentioned Anna to you? Ranas thinks she may have suffered some trauma on the ships."

His expression darkens. "Yes. A male she was close to, on the ships, tried to force-mate her."

Murderous thoughts enter my mind as anger churns deep in my gut. "Where is this male? Is he among the ones we rescued?" If he is, I will end him right now.

He shakes his head. "No. He died before the attack by the pirates." He places a hand on my shoulder. "But you must realize that this experience, along with the attack this day, has made her wary of all males. I do not blame her," he adds. "In her place, I would probably feel the same."

Raidyn steps forward. "Do the humans know that the Wind Clan had no intention of force-mating them?"

Varus's head snaps toward him. "How would they? All the humans understand is that they were almost taken against their will. Of course, they are afraid they would have been force-mated by your people. They do not understand that force-mating is a crime punishable by death on this world." He clenches his jaw. "We must make sure every Drakarian knows that abduction will not be tolerated either."

Raidyn hangs his head in shame. "My father and cousin have caused so much damage this day. Not just to your city, but also to our relationship with the humans. It will take a long time to repair."

He is right. I resolve to do whatever I can to convince Anna that I am a male of honor. One that would never harm her. One who is worthy of becoming her mate.

CHAPTER 9

ANNA

When I wake in the morning, I have a quick breakfast with Lilly and Talia. Prince Llyr and his sister, Noralla, left for their home in the Water Clan this morning. Skye and Raidyn have already returned to Wind Clan territory. Apparently, Raidyn needs to establish his rule now that he has taken over and his father is no longer King.

I worry for Skye, but from what I saw yesterday, Raidyn would die to protect her. Closing my eyes, I remember how he shielded her and took the fire from the blaster when John tried to kill her. If the shot hadn't torn through Raidyn's wing first, it would most likely have killed my friend.

When I first declined Kaj's advances, his reaction told me he is willing to do whatever it takes to convince me that I am his *linaya*. I'm worried that he might do something drastic if I reject him again. He seems like a good person, but I know all too well that looks can be deceiving.

I'm so lost in thought when I turn the corner to enter the

medical center that I nearly collide with Kaj. I lift my head and my eyes snag on the glowing fate mark swirling across the green scales on his chest.

"Are you all right?" he asks, his golden eyes full of concern.

"I'm fine. I just wasn't paying attention to where I was going."

His expression hardens. "You should always be mindful of your surroundings. It is dangerous to—"

I put my hand up to silence him. "You know what? I don't need you to tell me what to do, all right?"

"But I am your mate. It is my job to see that you are safe and protected," he argues.

I huff out a frustrated sigh. "You are *not* my mate."

He looks down at his chest, then back up at me, his brow furrowed deeply.

"And I don't care what that says." I gesture at the swirling mark on his chest. "*I* decide who I give my heart to. Not fate or some random cosmic force. Me." I point at my chest as I enunciate firmly. "*I* choose who I love. And you're not my mate until I say you are. Got it?"

I'm expecting him to argue, but instead, he straightens his shoulders and puffs out his chest as if trying to impress me. His nostrils flare as he stares down at me, his pupils blown wide so that only a thin golden line is visible around the edges. "Challenge accepted."

With that, he walks away, leaving me gaping. *"Challenge? What the hell?"*

Shaking my head, I walk over to Ranas, Kaj's cousin. He chuckles softly as I approach. "What's so funny?"

He arches a teasing brow. "I did not think you were interested in my cousin, and yet, you have challenged him to prove himself so you may judge his worth as a mate."

"What?" I ask, my voice rising in pitch. "I did no such thing. What are you talking about?"

He laughs. "Not all pairings are born of the fated bond, you know. When a male is interested in a female, she demands that he prove himself worthy to become hers. Just as you demanded of Kaj only a moment ago."

I'm at a loss. "What do you mean? I didn't ask him to prove himself."

"Yes, you did," he replies pointedly, a sly grin forming on his face. "I believe your exact words were, 'you're not my mate until I say you are.'"

My mouth drifts open, but I quickly snap it shut. "Oh my gosh." I put my head in my hands as I groan. "That's not what I meant."

I shadow Ranas for the first half of the morning, learning more about the various settings on the med scanner. The technology is amazing, but not as impressive as the healing fire Ranas can breathe on our patients. He was able to heal every remaining patient today with another application of fire.

I'm envious that I'll never be able to do this, but at least I can help. After all, the healing fire doesn't cure every ailment. I love still being able to work as a doctor on an alien world.

It's nearly time for the midday meal when Kaj finds me. He places a plate of food on my desk. I lift my gaze to thank him and he flashes a charming smile that stops my heart momentarily.

What the hell is wrong with me? Why am I reacting to him like this?

My cheeks flush with warmth and I quickly avert my eyes. "Thanks."

He tips his chin up with pride. "It is no burden to provide for my mate."

"I'm not your mate," I correct him.

"Not yet." He grins. "But you will be after I prove that I am a worthy male."

His expression is one of earnest sincerity. He's trying his best to please me, and aside from his insistence that we're fated to one another, he seems like a nice guy.

Alarms are practically blaring in the back of my mind. My fear insists that this is a trap like the one Edward set, but another part of me realizes that not every man is as evil as he was. If I spend the rest of my life comparing every man I come across to Edward, I'll always live in fear. I don't want that. I want to be happy. It's just so hard to trust this man, even *if* he claims he is my fated mate.

Another Healer offers me a cup of tea and Kaj growls low in his throat, causing the man to stumble backward and apologize quickly.

So that's one tick against him. He's overly possessive. It occurs to me that while Kaj may not be a rapist like Edward or John, he could be a crazy stalker.

When my shift is over, I head for the castle and he rushes to catch up to me, offering to fly me the rest of the way. I politely refuse; flying home in his arms would be too intimate.

I'm attracted to Kaj. All day, all he had to do was look my way and flash one of those handsome smiles and I started blushing like crazy.

He follows only a few steps behind me, and I realize this is his attempt at giving me space. That's yet another tick against him. He's looking more like a stalker by the second.

And yet, when I turn around and he gives me a beaming smile, my heart melts a bit.

When I reach the castle, I head straight for the gardens,

breathing a sigh of relief when Kaj doesn't follow. He's intelligent, charming and so handsome. I'm definitely attracted to him, but I need some space to really analyze our relationship. If this has any chance of working, we need to take things slowly. I need to be sure of the type of man he is before I allow myself to fall even more for him.

I love the palace gardens. It's my little sanctuary—beautiful and peaceful. With vibrant green trees and flowering bushes full of pink, yellow, and purple blossoms, this space is an oasis in the middle of the desert. A small stream winds along the path. I reach out and trace my fingers over one of the many hanging vines that sway gently in the dry desert breeze.

I don't want to complain because Varus and his people have been nothing but kind and helpful, but I never thought I would settle in a desert. There is a certain beauty to the sand, but it is not for me. I long for forests, winding rivers, and tall mountains. When I was a child, my parents and I would spend hours in the virtual reality room exploring the thick, forested mountains that used to exist on Earth before the trees were nearly all cut down by our ancestors.

Gravel crunches on the pathway behind me, and I turn to find Kaj. As soon as he notices my gaze on him, he dedicates obvious effort to pretending to study a blooming purple flower on a nearby bush. "Fascinating," he mumbles. "Almost as large as the koeli flower in the mountains."

"Mountains?" I ask, inwardly cursing myself when I realize I've spoken aloud.

His head snaps toward me. "Yes. In the Earth Clan territory."

Curiosity gets the best of me, and I can't help asking, "Varus mentioned there were some mountains there. Are there a lot of them?"

"Yes. Almost the entire terrain is mountainous. This

blossom," he points to the vivid flower, "is similar to a variety found near the peaks, called the koeli flower. The winds are strong that high up the mountains. During the harvest games, many males risk flying to the peaks to retrieve a koeli to prove their worth to a female they wish to mate."

I move to his side, studying it closely. It reminds me of a rose from Earth, but much larger.

"This is quite small compared to the koeli flowers, but the shape is very similar."

My eyes widen a fraction. This is the biggest flower I've ever seen, nearly as large as my fist, and he's calling it small? This one is gorgeous, and it makes me wonder what the koeli looks like if it is so rare that his clan has an annual game to search for it.

How romantic it would be to be given one… It sounds like an extreme version of the old Earth tradition of giving a woman flowers on a date.

"And this," he points to one of the trailing vines along the wall, "is lotae. It covers the walls of my castle." Though his eyes are on the verdant plant, his expression is far away.

"They're my favorite," I admit. The vine's blue flowers emit a soft glow at night, reminding me of glittering fairy lights I read about in stories as a child.

A hint of sadness flits across his features. "My sister, Rajila, brought these clippings to the palace the last time we came to visit and planted them here." A wistful smile curves his lips. "She and Varus's sister used to pick the blooms and turn them into woven necklaces and crowns for their hair."

"You have a sister?"

His eyes are bright with tears as they meet mine. "She died during the Great Plague. Along with Varus's sister, Laris."

I understand loss all too well. Wanting to offer him

comfort, I reach out and take his hand. "I'm sorry," I whisper. "You must miss her terribly."

He nods. "Every day."

"My parents and my younger sister died a few years ago when a virus broke out on the ships." I close my eyes against the pain. "I lost my entire family within a few days."

"My hearts grieve with yours."

"My heart grieves with you, as well."

He reaches out and picks one of the vibrant blue flowers then gently tucks it into my hair just above my ear. He smiles warmly, whispering, "Beautiful."

My cheeks flush with warmth. As I stare up at him, I realize it would be so easy to get lost in his golden eyes.

However, I don't want to rush into this. Clearing my throat, I lower my gaze and change the subject. "Lilly and Varus told me this morning that we're all going to the Water Clan territory for a peace celebration across Clans. I believe they called it the Summit—something your Clans used to do before the last Great War."

He nods. "It is truth. I can fly you there, if you'd like."

"You're not going home first?"

He shakes his head. "There is no need. I am only the prince. My parents take care of the kingdom. As heir to the throne, I represent them in foreign affairs."

Only the prince, he says, as if it's no big deal. I pin him with a glare. "You didn't tell me you were a prince. I had to find out from Lilly last night."

A sly smirk twists his lips. "You asked about me?"

I huff and roll my eyes in mock frustration. "No, I was just telling her about my day."

"I asked about you. And I learned a great deal about human females from Raidyn and Varus."

"What did—" I start to ask, but the sound of Lilly's voice cuts me off.

Kaj and I both turn in the same direction. Barely visible through the thick row of bushes, I watch Varus wrap his arms around Lilly from behind.

She cries out in surprise as he pulls her against his chest and nips at her ear. His voice is a low purr. "Shall we return to our rooms, my beautiful mate?"

Heat creeps up my neck and I quickly turn away, feeling as if I'm intruding on a private moment of theirs.

Kaj's eyes dart briefly to mine and a look of understanding passes between us. Quietly, we retreat into the castle. We ascend the stairs side by side and cross a long hallway. When I reach my room, he stops in front of the door with me.

He takes my hand and I lift my gaze to his, wondering what he means to do. "I enjoyed speaking with you this evening, Anna."

"So did I." The words leave my mouth before I can catch them. I watch another devastatingly handsome smile light his face. Inwardly, I curse myself for my unfiltered reply. Though what I said is true, I don't want to give him the wrong idea. I want to take things slow. Really slow. Someday, maybe I'll consider the mate thing.

He lifts my hand to his face and presses a tender kiss to the space between my thumb and forefinger. The brush of his lips across my skin makes my heart flutter.

"Until tomorrow," he whispers.

His golden eyes stare deep into mine. I'm so flustered that I can't think, much less form a coherent sentence to reply. "Uh... goodnight," I barely manage.

He sweeps down the hall as I step into my room. My heart is beating wildly in my chest. What's wrong with me? There's no denying I'm attracted to him, but I can't let him get under my skin like this. And certainly not so soon.

I make my way to the bathroom and peel off my robe as I

wade into the warm and inviting pool in the center of the room. For a city in a desert, there is an abundance of water here.

The cleansing rooms all come with showers and a bathing pool in the center of the space that could fit at least four people. Most of the pools are fed by warm springs, according to Lilly, but the rest use a superior water recycling technology that would have been so useful on our colony ships.

I release a deep sigh as I allow myself to float in the warm water. My time on the ships seems so very long ago. Almost like a completely different life.

When I'm finished bathing, I wrap myself in a robe and drop onto my bed. The thick, fluffy red comforter surrounds and envelopes me like a giant cloud. My eyes travel over the palatial room. With floating furniture carved of ornate, dark wood and several tapestries on the wall depicting Drakarians in *draka* form, the space reminds me of a medieval castle.

I wonder if each Clan's royal castle looks like this one. My thoughts drift again to Kaj. He's a prince, but I would never have known just by talking to him. He seems so... normal. He doesn't put on any airs. I close my eyes as I picture his face and that handsome smile. My body fills with warmth as I remember his lips brushing across my skin when he kissed my hand.

The image of him presenting himself to me and flexing his biceps floats to the surface of my mind. His entire body is covered in thick layers of corded muscle. He is masculine perfection incarnate.

Closing my eyes, I reach up and trace the hem of my robe, pulling it slightly open. I run my hand down my body, imagining the smooth, silken scales of his palms gliding over me.

A gentle breeze blows in through the open windows. The warm air skates across my skin, reminding me of when he breathed the soothing warmth of his healing fire across my shoulders and neck.

With a heavy sigh, I roll onto my side. I shouldn't be fantasizing about the man. There's no denying that I'm attracted to him, but I don't know him well enough to just accept that we're meant to be together. What happens if we don't work out? I doubt he'd be all right with just parting ways.

That's where my true fear lies. I remember the day I told Edward I didn't want to see him anymore. It was the worst day of my life. The last thing I want is to walk into a situation like that again.

I may have only just recently met him, but I can't imagine that Kaj is abusive. At least, that's what my romantic heart keeps insisting, even as my brain insists that I remain cautious.

Closing my eyes, I picture his face and the way he stared at me so intensely as he kissed the back of my hand. I reach up and touch my lips, imagining what his mouth might feel like on mine.

With a heavy sigh, I fluff the pillow up under my head, mentally chastising myself once again. The image of Kaj's face fills my thoughts as I drift off to sleep.

CHAPTER 10

KAJ

I lie awake in bed, staring at the ceiling. My mate is in the room beside mine.

So close, yet so far away.

I asked Varus to give me the bedroom connected to hers, and he reluctantly obliged. He told me she might be displeased if she knew, though I do not understand why. It is my job as her mate to watch over and protect her. If any dare try to disturb her sleep, I will be the first to know.

My nostrils flare as her delicate scent seeps into the room. Even with the door between our two rooms closed, I can sense it thickening.

"Kaj!" She cries out my name.

Alarm bursts through me. I jerk up in bed and rush through the door to find her tangled in the sheets. Her eyes are wide and a fine sheen of perspiration glimmers across the pink tone of her skin.

"What is wrong?"

She tugs the blanket around her body, shielding her

naked skin from my gaze. Anger joins the shock flashing in her eyes. "What are you doing here?"

I cock my head to the side. "You called out for me only a moment ago. I thought you were in distress."

Her cheeks turn a deeper shade of red than I've ever seen on a human. "I was... dreaming," she finally says.

"Of me?"

She lowers her gaze, piquing my interest. The scent of her need is so strong it is maddening. My linaya was dreaming of me, and I am curious to know what I was doing in her dreams. My voice comes out like a purr. "What were you dreaming of, Anna?"

"Nothing," she snaps, obviously flustered. "Get out. You shouldn't be in here. Where did you even come from, anyway?" Her gaze drifts to the open doorway between our rooms and her jaw drops. "You came from in there?" She points accusingly to the door.

I nod. "I asked Varus to give me the room beside yours in case you needed me. I cannot allow another to care for you when that is my duty as your mate, even if you have not declared my success in your challenge."

She looks indignant, pointing again to the door. "I don't need anyone. I already told you that. Now, get out."

I realize my mistake. She believes I am hovering over her. Drakarian females do not like an overly possessive male, and it seems that my mate feels the same. However, I cannot help but seek her out. Even without the fate mark, I would pursue her. I watched her when we treated patients after the attack. She is as brilliant as she is beautiful, and I long to know more about Anna.

But as she glares at me, I realize that I will never get this chance if I do not acquiesce now. She wishes for privacy, and I must grant it. Now that I know she is not in distress, I have no reason to be here.

I bow low. "Forgive me. When you called for me, I was worried, but you are obviously well. I will leave you alone."

With difficulty, I force myself to turn and walk away from her. I return to my room, looking over my shoulder as I close the door quietly behind me. With a heavy sigh, I scrub my hand across my face.

I do not know what to do. How can I prove to her that I am worthy to be her mate when she doesn't even want me near?

CHAPTER 11

KAJ

A nna has avoided me for the past few days and I have forced myself to give her some space. But today we leave for the Water Clan territory to attend the peace celebration. I am eager to see her and hope she will wish to ride on my back for the journey. I will not pressure her, however—I will merely offer to carry her there.

The travel party has already shifted into draka form. At least a dozen warriors line up in formation, readying to take flight. I watch as Varus's mate climbs onto his back and settles between his shoulders. He gently nuzzles her with his snout. How I envy him his relationship. He adores his mate, and it is obvious to see that she loves him equally in return.

I scan the rest of the females gathered but do not see Anna. Worry fills me. I did not anticipate this. If she has decided to stay behind, I will make an excuse to stay here as well, for I cannot bear the thought of parting from my linaya.

I smile as soon as I see her emerge from the castle and enter the courtyard. She is walking beside Ranas and they are heading straight toward me. Nervous anticipation buzzes through my veins as I wait for her approach.

I hope she finds my draka form appealing. This is the first time she has seen it. I glance around at the other males. My green scales are practically sparkling beneath the bright sun. I took great care to buff them this morning to a fine sheen, hoping to impress her.

Varus stops beside me, squinting. "Could you please step into the shade?"

I cock my head to the side. "Why?"

"Because you are going to blind all of us with your shining scales."

I narrow my eyes at him, and he laughs. "I merely jest, my friend." He looks me up and down. "You appear regal this day. I'm sure your female will be impressed." He turns to his mate on his shoulders. "What do you think, my linaya?"

She smiles. "Anna loves the color green, so you definitely have that going for you."

I look down at myself. This is good. Members of the Earth Clan have scales in varying shades of green and brown. I have always considered myself blessed to have inherited my father's coloring, a rich shade of green that nearly matches the great trees of the forest.

I puff my chest out and tip up my chin as I wait for Anna to approach, hoping she will think me *regal*, as Varus said.

The humans wanted to revive an old Earth custom full of dancing, food, drink, and merriment—a ball, they call it. According to Lilly, a ball requires a certain code of dress. As I study my mate, I find that I appreciate this custom they have introduced.

Anna is dressed in a long, flowing green gown that sways gently around her ankles with every step. I am pleased to notice the color nearly matches my scales, and I wonder if she chose this on purpose.

The neckline bares the delicate form of her shoulders and dips in a small *V* just above the valley of her breasts. The top of the softly curved mounds peeks just above the neckline of the fabric. Her long, brown hair is twisted up in an intricate hairstyle, exposing the elegant column of her neck. The wind blows gently around her, carrying her delicious scent on the breeze. I inhale deeply, relishing my mate's fragrance.

My hearts hammer as her gaze travels over me appreciatively. She is appraising me in my draka form just as a Drakarian female would. I have heard the human females are in awe of our ability to transform, so I hope Anna feels the same.

"Good morning, Kaj." She smiles warmly.

"Good morning, Anna," I reply with the standard human greeting. "Would you like me to carry you for our journey?"

She shakes her head and then looks to my cousin. "No. Thank you, though. I'll just go with Ranas."

My expression falls. "Of—of course." I bite back my disappointment.

A sharp stab of jealousy rips through me as Ranas transforms and wraps his tail around her waist, lifting her onto his back. I narrow my eyes at him, a small puff of smoke escaping my nostrils. He has the decency to look guilty, at least.

Once she is settled between his shoulders, he moves closer to me as we ready to take off. He leans forward and whispers in a voice so low I am certain she is unable to hear it. "Forgive me. How could I say no when she asked me this morning?"

"Very easily," I counter, narrowing my eyes.

He snorts out a laugh.

A small human female approaches me. She looks familiar, but I cannot place how I know her. "Could you give me a ride?" she asks in a small voice.

"Of course," I reply. I would never deny a female aid.

She beams. "Thanks. I'm Holly. What's your name?"

I bow low. "I am Kaj. It is pleasing to meet you, Holly."

Rakan—Varus's personal guard—moves up beside me. He growls low, and I arch a questioning brow as I turn to him. My eyes widen slightly when I realize he is jealous.

"Mine," he mouths as he looks to the female, climbing up onto my back. I am surprised by both his aggression and his twisted expression, but then again, I remember my reaction only a moment ago to my cousin.

I dip my chin in subtle acknowledgment. If he desires this pale-skinned, blonde-haired female, what do I care? I do not want her. I desire only Anna.

The female on my back seems nervous and I turn back to reassure her. "Do not worry. I will not let you fall."

She smiles. "Thanks."

I narrow my eyes at Ranas, who stands beside me with my mate on his back. She leans over, completely oblivious to my gaze as she chats with Lilly and Varus.

"Traitor," I whisper to him.

"I am nothing of the sort," he whispers, chortling. "And you know it."

I growl low. This is going to be a very long flight.

CHAPTER 12

ANNA

Holly climbs onto Kaj's back. I can't hear their conversation, but she smiles at him, and I watch as he returns the smile then laughs. A puff of smoke escapes his nostrils, and he shakes his head. She leans forward to rest the length of her body against him.

Bitter acid rises in my throat. What the hell is she doing? She told me just yesterday that she had a crush on Rakan. And yet, she didn't ask *him* for a ride. When I glance at him next to Kaj, I see no one on his back.

Mentally, I chastise myself. Why am I jealous? I have no reason to be. It's not like I've staked a claim on Kaj. We're not together, even though he insists we should be. In fact, Holly's advances could be a good thing. Maybe he'll forget about the fated-mates nonsense and move on.

At least... that's what I'm trying to convince myself of anyway.

As we fly across the desert plains, I observe Kaj and Holly

laughing and chatting. I keep telling myself this is good, but my heart keeps insisting otherwise.

I force myself to focus on the ground below, watching the desert plains give way to green fields and hills lush with vegetation. It's such a strange and striking contrast to the Fire Clan lands, making me long to explore more of this world.

The air grows cooler, and I peer ahead, my mouth drifting open in wonder at a vast blue ocean. We make a wide arc over the sea, and I smile as I watch a school of fish racing beneath the water. Giant waves crash against the cliff wall below an enormous castle. White towers proudly reach toward the blue sky. The silver-capped domes gleam beneath the sun, reminiscent of the Fire Clan castle.

We land in the center of a courtyard overgrown with vivid flowering plants. Ranas touches down so lightly I don't even know we've landed until he wraps his tail around my waist to gently lower me to the ground. I turn to thank him but trail off in awe as the dragons transform back into humanoid form.

Kaj's eyes are heavy on me for a moment before I turn back to the castle. Something in his expression sends a shiver down my spine, and even now, I can feel his gaze boring into my back.

I force a smile onto my face as Talia and Lilly rush to my side, bursting with excitement.

"It's so beautiful here." Talia smiles "Isn't it?"

"It is," I agree. "It makes me curious to see what the other Clans' territories look like."

Lilly chimes in, "What's going on with you and Kaj? Are you ignoring him?"

I lower my gaze. "Sort of," I admit. "It's just…" I trail off, hesitant to voice my fears.

"Just what?" she presses, nudging my side.

"I'm attracted to him, but that scares me."

"Why?" Her eyes widen first in surprise, then narrow. "He didn't do anything to make you uncomfortable, did he? Varus told him to court you, not insist that you are his—like Raidyn apparently did with Skye."

"No. He hasn't. It's not that." I sigh and glance around to make sure no one is listening. "Don't you think that it's all happening too fast? Them, us, and this fated mates business?"

"That's how the fate mark works, according to Varus." She smiles reassuringly, gesturing to her mate. "Look at us; I only knew him a few days before I was head over heels and already agreeing to be his."

"What if Kaj is like…"

I don't even have to finish my question because she already knows what I mean to say. *What if he's like Edward?*

She shakes her head, pity in her eyes. "Varus claims that Kaj would never do what Edward did."

I sigh heavily because I know all my doubts and fears are running rampant in my mind. If I allow them to, they will consume my life. I don't want that. I would rather find happiness and learn to trust again. It would be so easy to just surrender to my blooming feelings for Kaj, but I'm worried I might find we aren't a good match. Would he respect my decision and let me go? Part of me doubts that, especially because of the fated bond.

She meets my eyes evenly. "Do you like him?"

"I don't know," I lie. The truth is I do like him, but the idea of becoming his lifelong mate is overwhelming. "You really need to talk to Varus about our room arrangements in his castle."

Her brow wrinkles. "What do you mean?"

I huff. "He put Kaj in the room right next to mine, and he came bursting through the door a few nights ago."

Her eyes widen. "He did?"

"Yeah. It startled me, to say the least."

"Why didn't you tell me sooner?"

I roll my eyes. "Um... maybe because you and Varus have been all over each other the past few days, so we haven't had a chance to talk."

A dark blush spreads across her cheeks. "He says my scent is driving him mad," she mumbles, a smile tugging at her lips.

"Your scent?"

She shrugs. "Apparently, it's stronger now that I'm pregnant."

In my study of Drakarian medical literature, I've read about the importance of scent marking to their culture. The biological compulsion to mark their mates helps alert others that they are mated.

She clears her throat. "Anyway, I don't think you'll have to worry about the room situation anymore."

"Why?"

"Because I'm pretty sure he's going home after this gathering." Her smile grows sad. "Back to the Earth Clan lands. Those rooms were only temporary since his Clan sent Healers to help with the aftermath of the invasion. Now that everyone is healed, Healer Ranas will be able to handle things again."

"Thank goodness," I tell her, feigning relief. Deep down, an uncomfortable knot forms in the pit of my stomach at the thought of him leaving.

Stars, I'm such a mess. Why does this have to be so hard? Why can't I be more like Talia? I know that the second the glowing fate mark appears on Llyr's chest, she'll jump into his arms. But I keep letting my fears and doubts get the best of me.

Varus walks up to Lilly. She immediately loops her arm with his. He leans down and places a tender kiss on her temple, and my heart melts. I'm so happy for my friend. I dart a glance to the side and find Kaj staring straight at me, his expression speaking volumes.

That could be us... if I only accept him.

I sigh heavily. I could have what Lilly has. I wish I could find a way to shut off the part of my mind that harbors doubt. I turn away and follow Lilly and Talia into the castle.

My jaw drops when we enter the large ballroom. Floor-to-ceiling windows line the far wall, with a gorgeous view of the deep-blue ocean. A floating chandelier above casts a soft glow throughout the entire space, highlighting the intricate tile inlay on the floor depicting great, swirling images of the sea.

The layout is open and airy, built in a sleek and elegant design. Although the Drakarians are a highly advanced species, they also have a love of beautiful things that is evident in all the intricately carved furnishings they use in their decorations and furniture.

A long table on one side of the ballroom is overflowing with food and drinks. Tall, fluted glasses with pink bubbling liquid draw my eye. Is that this world's version of champagne? I approach the table and lift a glass to my nose, sniffing.

My mouth waters at the sweet citrusy smell, and I take a small sip. The liquid rolls across my tongue in a burst of delightful exotic flavor, with a hint of strawberries and oranges. This is the best drink I've tried on this world so far.

Ranas walks up beside me. "What is this?" I hold the glass out to him.

"It is a celebratory beverage," he explains. "Fermented fruit with a hint of spice."

"So, it's like alcohol?"

He cocks his head to the side in question and I realize I need to explain.

"It alters the mind, right? Creates a state of euphoria?"

He nods. "Yes. Something like that. We verified that it is safe for human consumption, but it is best to drink in moderation only."

To be honest, I've never been much of a drinker. We had alcohol on the ships, but I never liked the taste. I love this stuff, however. I finish my first glass then pick up another. I'm already starting to like this celebration.

I watch in wonder as couples pair off and glide across the dance floor. This is how I always imagined a ball would be. It's beautiful and elegant and completely magical. The Drakarians are awkward dancers, but their human partners don't seem to care. This is more fun than we've had in a long time.

On the ships, everything was about survival. There always seemed to be one crisis or another to solve. On this world, it feels like we can finally breathe a sigh of relief for the first time and really enjoy ourselves.

As I watch the humans and Drakarians mingle together, at peace, I realize that this new normal may be better than what we'd originally anticipated when our people set out on the colony ships to search for a new world.

Since the Drakarians are so willing to help us, our survival shouldn't be a problem here. Aside from the Wind Clan attack, they seem to be kind people. Working alongside Ranas and interacting with other Drakarians, I've learned that I shouldn't judge the whole species by a few bad people. Just as they shouldn't judge us for the misdeeds of a few hostile humans—like John. He was just as bad as Edward and we didn't realize it until it was nearly too late.

Thank the Stars Raidyn came along when he did and saved Skye.

Ranas smiles as he walks up to me, pulling me back from my dark thoughts. He offers me another glass of champagne.

I really shouldn't take it; I've already had four glasses. However, I feel so relaxed, I figure another glass can't hurt.

We sit quietly together as I finish my drink. When I'm done, he stands and extends his hand to me with a small bow.

"Would you like to dance?"

I smile. "Sure." Ranas is a good guy, and we're just friends. There's no pressure here, so why not enjoy myself? Besides, I've always wanted to dance at a ball since I first read about them in Earth's ancient history books.

We're not even halfway to the dance floor when I suddenly bump into a rather large chest. I lift my eyes and find Kaj looking down at me. He glares at Ranas while a growl builds in his throat. We're so close that the vibrations move through me, sending a spike of heat straight to my core. Only now do I realize that my hand is on his chest, directly over the beautiful, swirling fate mark. Is it strange that I love that it shines only for me?

"Mine," I whisper to myself. I inhale sharply and place my hand over my mouth when I realize I've spoken this aloud.

"Yours," he agrees in a low, rumbling purr.

Desire pools deep in my core as his eyes heat. My mind floats in a state of euphoria. I'm lost in his golden gaze as he pulls me onto the dance floor. We whirl and spin and I'm surprised by how wonderfully he dances compared to the other Drakarian men.

Despite his heavily muscled form, he moves with such grace. "Where did you learn how to dance?" I ask.

"From one of the other humans," he replies. "I knew this ball was important to you and your people. So I wanted to learn all that I could about this custom before we came here."

Jealousy fills me at the thought of him dancing with another woman, but it's quickly tempered when he explains his reasoning. He really is a thoughtful man. I really should give him a chance. After all, why am I fighting this? Especially when being this close to him feels so good.

With his chest pressed against mine and his hand around my waist, I feel safe instead of trapped. Protected and cherished instead of in danger. The beautiful twinkling lights of the chandelier above are casting a lovely iridescent glow upon his green scales. He is the most handsome man I've ever seen. Green has always been my favorite color and as I look to him, I wonder if this was fate like he believes.

I place my hand on his chest, over the lovely glowing fate mark. "You are so handsome," I murmur. "I could just kiss you right now."

His eyes flare with heat. "You wish to kiss me?"

Unable to speak, I nod.

Without hesitation, he lifts me into his arms and carries me bridal-style onto a balcony overlooking the sea. He sets me back on my feet, staring down at me intensely. The waves crash along the cliff wall below, sending a fine spray of mist up to where we're standing. He moves in front of me, shielding me from this and it's such a gentlemanly thing to do, my heart skips a beat.

It occurs to me that he doesn't know how to kiss. After all, Lilly and Skye said it's not something Drakarians normally do. And their mates were both surprised by this act.

I stretch up on my toes and wrap my arms around Kaj's neck. Reaching up, I gently trace my fingers across his lips. I imagined touching him like this in my dreams last night. They're soft like silk, and I wonder what it would be like to kiss him. Will it be as wonderful as I dreamed?

Cautiously, I lean in and press my lips to his. He stills as if he's not sure what to do. Finally, he opens his mouth, and his tongue curls around mine. He explores my mouth slowly and gently at first, growing more intense by the second.

He tastes of earth and cinnamon. His ridged tongue drags deliciously against mine as he deepens and takes control of our kiss. What he lacks in experience, he makes up for with passion. I moan as he strokes in and out of my mouth, wondering where he learned how to kiss so well.

I run my hands down his back, kneading the muscles of his neck and shoulders. His scales are warm and smooth beneath the tips of my fingers. My nipples prick against the fabric of my dress as he presses his chest to mine. I've never wanted anyone as much as I want him at this moment.

I take his hand and place his palm over my breast. He rips his mouth from mine, and I notice his pupils are blown wide in a hungry gaze. "Not here, my beautiful mate. I will take you to my kingdom and claim you there. Do you accept me? Do you wish to be mine?"

More than anything. Why have I been fighting this so hard? I want Kaj.

"Yes. Take me," I whisper, my body humming with longing.

Without hesitation, he shifts into his *draka* form then scoops me up in his taloned hand. We lift into the air, flying out to sea. His wings billow like great sails as he dips low then turns back toward land, following the cliffs along the shoreline.

Every fiber of my body is still thrumming with need. "Hurry," I breathe. "I need you."

He pumps his wings furiously as he picks up speed.

"How far away is your kingdom?"

"Not far," he replies. "Sleep, my mate. You will need your rest. For when I claim you, I will take you many times and for several days."

My thighs squeeze together involuntarily at his words. Why did I ever fight this? I can't remember now.

I don't want to sleep just yet, but watching the coastline

fly by, my eyelids start to flutter with exhaustion, so I decide to rest for a bit. Closing my eyes, I fall into darkness, dreaming of his touch. I hope my first time is as wonderful as I've always imagined.

CHAPTER 13

KAJ

My hearts soar. She has agreed to be mine. I could have claimed her at the Water Clan's castle, but she is to be my princess, and some day, my queen. It is Earth Clan tradition to take one's mate to a secluded dwelling deep in the forest for the first mating. I will not deny my mate this tradition, especially since the gods favor such matings, increasing the chances of conception.

A low growl vibrates my chest at the thought of filling my mate with my essence. I will take her over and over again beneath the stars, allowing the gods to look upon us and bless our coupling. I will bind her to me in all ways so that every male will know without a doubt that she is mine.

Forever seems to pass until we cross over into Earth territory. I feel as if my land is welcoming me home. The fresh, earthy scent of the forest below drifts on the cool breeze that sweeps over the mountains. Anna will be pleased,

I believe, to live here. The terrain is mountainous, plentiful in both water and vegetation. The forests are thick and full of life. My lands are the near opposite of the Fire territory.

I have prepared a nest specifically for when I take a mate, as all Earth Clan males do. It took two cycles to construct with my own hands. I hope she will be impressed with my efforts. The house is nestled high up in the mountains, near a cascading waterfall.

I built the structure from solid beams of dark k'lor and hand-carved detailed nature scenes into the wood inside. I hope she is happy with all the attention I dedicated to making this space comfortable for our nest.

I land on the upper balcony and quickly shift forms. My mate is asleep, so I carefully carry her in through the double glass doors. The bed is expansive and covered in only the finest fabrics, soft and lush. I carefully pull back the covers and lay her gently down beneath the blankets.

I scan her clothing, wondering if I should remove it so she may sleep comfortably. However, I remember Varus's comments about how uncomfortable humans are with nudity. Unlike my people, they prefer to stay clothed.

Even though I think the custom strange, I decide against undressing her and instead crawl into bed beside her sleeping form. She has already spent days resisting our mating bond because she was afraid of the speed at which my people fall in love. I consider how far she has outrun the darkness of her past and know that I must do everything in my power to ensure that she does not regress because of my actions.

I desire more than anything to claim her, but my linaya is sleeping, and I refuse to wake her. If she wants to mate with me, she must be the one to make the first move. She has agreed to be mine. That is enough for now.

Slowly, I curl myself protectively around her smaller

form and wrap my arm around her waist. I pull her back against me and bury my nose in her hair, inhaling deeply of her delicate scent.

"Mine," I whisper against the shell of her ear as I close my eyes and allow myself to drift away.

CHAPTER 14

ANNA

My head is throbbing as I slowly return to awareness. My skin is so warm I must have a fever. Slowly, I open my eyes. Sunlight assaults my vision as I squint against the blinding light. Oh Stars, I feel awful.

I shift, and something tightens around my waist. I freeze, only my eyes glancing around frantically. My mouth drifts open when I notice a scaled, green arm wrapped around me. Something hard presses insistently against my backside, and although I've never felt one before, I think I recognize a *stav* —as the Drakarians call their manhood.

I swallow thickly. Oh, Stars. At least I'm still fully clothed. I blink several times, trying to figure out the best way to untangle myself here. Anger rises, but I suppress it when a foggy memory floats to the front of my mind. I remember making out with Kaj on a balcony. He asked me if I wanted to move to his palace and become his mate. I remember the feel of his mouth on mine and his hands caressing my skin.

My brain was swimming in champagne at the time while my body was practically screaming for him to take me right there. I said yes—I remember that part very clearly.

My gaze scans the room. We're sleeping in what looks like a cabin built by ancient Vikings. The walls are constructed from several thick logs, the wood carved in intricate and beautiful patterns. Tapestries decorate the walls with images of Drakarians in *draka* form and plush gray rugs line the floor. On the wall directly across from me, a space has been hollowed out and surrounded by large rocks to make a fireplace, the hearth stacked with strange crystals and wood.

Drawing in a deep breath, I slowly turn to face Kaj. His eyes are closed, and he's still asleep. With his warm body pressed against mine, I inhale a deep breath of his masculine scent, a heady mix of earth and cinnamon.

It would be so easy to just give in to his advances, but I'm afraid of moving too fast. Drakarians don't do casual relationships. When they mate, it's forever.

I'm going to ask him to take me back to the Water Clan castle. My friends were planning to stay there for the next several days. I didn't tell anyone where I've gone or even that I was leaving. I'm sure they will worry if we don't return soon.

He opens his eyes with a sleepy smile. He leans in and places a tender kiss on my forehead as he brushes the hair back from my face. "Good morning, my beautiful mate."

His golden eyes regard me as if I were the best thing that ever happened to him.

That's why this conversation is going to be so hard.

I smile nervously. "Kaj, I need you to take me back to the Water Clan castle."

"But we just got here," he mutters, scanning my face as his brow furrows deeply. "We have not yet sealed our bond."

He traces his hand from my shoulder down my arm, then entwines our fingers. He lifts our joined hands to his lips and presses a kiss to the back of my hand. Heat pools deep in my core as his gaze holds mine. His nostrils flare and he growls low in arousal. "I can scent your need, my linaya."

He leans in and presses his lips to mine. They're as soft and warm as I remember. He cups the back of my head and pulls me closer as his tongue enters my mouth. The hard ridges stroke against my tongue in a delicious give and take.

I moan as he wraps his other arm tightly around my back and tugs me closer, deepening our kiss. His *stav* is a hard bar against my thigh, and when he rolls his hips, he shifts until it's pressed against my folds. The only thing separating us is the thin fabric of my dress.

I want him so badly, but I know we should stop.

I place my palm to his chest and gently push him away. He studies me with a questioning look. "What is wrong, my Anna?"

"I'm sorry, Kaj. I—I can't do this. We need to return to the Water Clan castle."

"But you said you were mine."

"I know, and I'm sorry. I had too much of that drink last night and it clouded my judgment. It was a mistake to come here with you."

He stills. His eyes flash with hurt. With a clenched jaw, he pulls away from me and climbs off the bed. He turns his back to me, and I brace myself, waiting to see what he'll do. After a moment, he finally rasps, "Very well. If that is what you wish, I will take you back."

I'm shocked. "You will?"

He turns to me, shoulders slumped. "Yes."

He's willing to take me back simply because I asked. Maybe he's not like Edward at all. I stand and move toward him. "Thank you for understanding, Kaj."

"I will no longer bother you," he adds dejectedly. "Once I have taken you back, I will return to my territory."

My heart stops. I may not be entirely sure about us, but that doesn't mean I feel nothing. I don't want him to leave me. "You don't have to go just because of me," I offer. "I—"

His smile is pained. "I am needed here. And... in truth, it is difficult to be around you when you do not want me." Absently, he places a hand on his chest, directly over the swirling fate mark. "It is something I will learn to accept. I will not pressure you into taking me as yours."

His words touch something deep inside me. "It's not that I don't want you, Kaj, because I do." His eyes light with hope, so I rush to continue. "It's just that we're moving a bit fast and I—I want to be sure that we're compatible. That we won't end up killing each other one day."

He stares at me, aghast. "I would never harm you. My vow. Females are cherished and treasured among my kind and—"

I laugh softly and place a finger on his lips to silence him. "It's just a figure of speech." I grin. "I don't mean that we'd literally kill each other. Just that we might argue a lot and be miserable."

His brows draw down. "I want only to please you."

"I know," I sigh. He has made this point multiple times. "But—"

I stutter to a halt. I have to tell him the truth, no matter how painful. Drawing in a deep and steadying breath, I face him and admit, "I have a hard time trusting people. Men, specifically. I was..." I swallow against the lump in my throat. "A guy I was close to... tried to hurt me."

His golden gaze holds mine as he waits patiently for me to continue.

"His actions made me afraid to get involved with anyone because I don't want that to happen again."

As the words leave my mouth, I realize I'm relieved to get this off my chest. I rarely talk about the assault, but Kaj needs to know. I want him to understand exactly why I am hesitant to accept him.

He takes my hand and places it on his hearts. "I would sooner end my life than ever harm you, Anna. I would do anything to make you happy. Please. Allow me to prove that I would be a good mate to you, that I am an honorable male. Will you give me this chance?"

My brain is telling me to be cautious, but my heart—the hopeless romantic—is practically screaming at me to say yes. He's a good guy who has never given me a reason to distrust him. He asked me if I wanted to come here, and he's willing to take me back to my friends should I ask. So far, he has forced nothing upon me.

I meet his reflective golden eyes. "All right. Let's give us a chance."

CHAPTER 15

KAJ

Us. She said *us*. My hearts soar and I want nothing more than to take her in my arms and shower her with human kisses. I barely stop myself in time to realize that I must allow her to lead. She feels that the fate bond has been forced upon her and must decide if she wants to accept—if she wishes to claim me as her mate or reject me.

Her green eyes look lost. "What now?"

I cock my head to the side. I had not considered the future. If she were a Drakarian female, we would already be mating. Repeatedly. But she is human, and their ways are different, so I need to be cautious and deliberate before I act on my feelings. "What would you like to do?"

Her cheeks flush a lovely shade of red as she softly bites her lower lip. "Well... maybe we could just stay here. Spend time getting to know one another better."

She wishes to spend time with me. This is good, for my first choice is obviously to stay here, without contending with the constant interruption of other people. Surely, we can grow closer during long hours of shared time and conversation. "You wish to stay here?" I ask, just to be certain.

"Yes." She smiles. Her voice radiates more confidence. "We should stay. But I think we should let everyone know where we are. Don't you think?"

I lower my gaze. "I did not install a communication center here."

"Why not?"

"Because this was meant to be a place that is undisturbed from the outside world."

"Oh," she replies. "Like a getaway place?"

I frown for I do not understand this term.

She explains. "A place to relax."

I do not tell her it was built expressly as a nest for my future mate because I worry it would make her feel uncomfortable. So instead, I nod. "Yes. That is a good way to describe it."

She looks to me. "Did people see us leave together?"

"Yes. There were many nearby when we were on the balcony. That is why I suggested going somewhere more private."

"Then, they know I'm with you, so they shouldn't be worried. It's not like you stole me away or anything."

"We can travel to the castle and contact them from there," I offer.

She shrugs. "All right. But first, I'd like to explore a bit. I've never been somewhere like this before. What is there to do around here?"

My gaze immediately darts to the bed, the sole reason I constructed this nest. I built the house with the intent of bringing my female here for our first mating, followed by many more, but she is not ready to mate just yet. I look over her shoulder out the window, glimpsing the forest around us.

"You expressed a love of the mountains and woods. We can go anywhere you wish."

She beams. "That would be wonderful."

"Then, let us go." I gesture to the door.

Her expression falls as her gaze travels down my form. "Could you maybe put on some clothes?"

I arch a questioning brow. "Does my appearance bother you?"

Although I force my expression to remain impassive, on the inside, I am nervous that she will confirm my fears. If she finds my appearance unappealing, she will never desire to mate with me. I glance down at my green scales. I always thought them a lovely deep shade, but perhaps she prefers the orange-and-red coloring of the Fire Clan. Or the Water Clan's varying shades of purple and blue. If so, there is absolutely nothing I can do to change her mind. It is not as if I could will my scales to change color.

But... I may be able to paint myself. I believe our ancestors used to apply dyes and such to indicate Clan markings. My people have not done this in hundreds of cycles, but I would be willing to do so if she asked.

Varus and Raidyn were the ones who suggested that I buff my scales to a fine sheen. They said their human mates appreciated their shining scales. However, I am now thinking that isn't enough. I may have to paint myself an entirely different color.

"Yes," she finally replies and my hearts sink.

If dyeing or polishing my scales does not work, I will die old and alone. I will never know the joys of having a mate by my side or in my bed. Already, I am envisioning the hermit I will become if she rejects me, for I could never consider taking another as mine—not when I've already met the most perfect of all females in existence.

"But not because I think you're ugly," she adds quickly.

My ears perk up. "You're not. But I—I'd feel more comfortable if you were dressed."

She lowers her gaze to the ground and tucks a stray tendril of hair behind her ear in what I recognize as a nervous gesture. "Humans only get naked around someone else to bathe or to... mate."

"Ah." Understanding dawns. She is worried because of her trauma that I may try to force myself upon her. I move quickly to reassure her. "So, until you are ready to mate, you wish for me to remain clothed?" I ask, just to be certain I've understood her.

"Ummm... sure," she hedges, slightly hesitant.

"This is easily done."

Her shoulders sag in relief. "Oh, good. I'm glad you understand."

I nod firmly. "But you must let me know when you wish for me to disrobe again."

Her lips part and her expression makes me wonder if I have done something wrong. I'm about to ask when she shakes off her expression and replies, "All right. I'll uh... I'll definitely do that."

Now that I have settled her concerns, a thought occurs to me. If I am to entice her to become my mate, I should first impress her with the nest I have built. "Before we leave, allow me to give you a tour."

She nods.

"This," I gesture grandly to the space around us, "is the bedroom."

She does not appear impressed, so I decide to offer more insight into my process of construction and decoration.

"I built this structure myself. It took me many days to hand-carve all of the furnishings within, but I believe they turned out rather well."

Her eyes widen as she surveys the room, and I struggle to

hold back a smile, interpreting her expression as awestricken. "You did all this yourself?" she asks, astonishment coloring her tone.

"Yes."

She runs her hands reverently over the carefully carved chair beside her. "It's beautiful, Kaj."

"Thank you. I am glad that it pleases you." Dipping my chin in a subtle bow, I turn and gesture to a door across the room. "Through there is the cleansing room."

When she opens the door, she gasps. "You have a full pool for bathing here?"

"It is standard in Drakarian cleansing rooms," I explain. Although I neglect to mention that I built mine larger than average since I enjoy long, hot baths at the end of the day. Now that she is standing so close to the edge of the pool, I imagine us both sitting in the water. Me, lathering soap across her delicate skin as she rewards me with more human kisses.

I push down my wandering thoughts and lead her into the kitchen and living area downstairs. A thick green rug covers the cold floors before our wide fireplace. Varus told me his mate finds mating on a soft surface before a fireplace very romantic.

So, after I put my mate to bed last night, I moved the largest, thickest rug I could find in front of the fireplace in case she wishes to mate there.

The wooden furnishings are covered with matching plush green cushions, including the long L-shaped sofa that faces both the fireplace and the wall of windows that overlook the forested mountains. I have built a firepit here in the courtyard reminiscent of the one in Varus's gardens.

I noticed the humans have a fondness for gathering around the fire in Varus's palace, so perhaps Anna will enjoy it here as well. "I thought we could make a fire this evening if you'd like." I gesture to the firepit outside the window.

She smiles. "That would be great. I love sitting around a fire."

This is good. My instincts were right.

The kitchen is equipped with the finest stasis unit for storing food and the highest-quality appliances for cooking. The long gray countertop that separates the kitchen from the living area lends an open flow to the entire space that I hope she enjoys.

As if reading my thoughts, she traces her fingers over the counter. "Is this wood?"

"Yes. I cut it from a felled tree that I found in the forest. It is sealed, so it is waterproof and will not stain if that is your concern," I offer, picturing making her meals as she watches me lovingly, asking for samples of my cooking.

She smiles. "No, I just think it looks beautiful."

Pride fills me. She appreciates my fine craftsmanship. "I am pleased you like it."

Her gaze sweeps to the appliances. "I don't know how to use these. Could you show me later?"

I'm aghast at the suggestion. Does she believe I will not prepare her food? It is a Drakarian male's duty to provide the meals for his mate and family. "You do not need to worry about them," I tell her. "I will provide for you."

"Thank you, but I... I actually enjoy cooking. I'd like to try my hand at it here."

This is surprising. "Do your males not prepare and serve food to their mates?"

She laughs. "Uh... usually, it's the other way around."

I arch a brow.

"Wait. Are you saying that Drakarian *men* are supposed to cook all the meals for the family?" she asks incredulously.

"Yes, it is a male's duty to tend to his mate in all ways. He is also the primary caretaker of the fledglings."

She gapes at me.

I puff my chest out with pride. "That is why a male must prove himself in all ways to his mate. He must be strong enough to protect and provide for her and any fledglings they may have."

She surveys the kitchen. "I'd still like to learn how to cook for myself. All right?"

If this is what she desires, who am I to argue? "Of course. We shall prepare the mid-day meal together."

She smiles up at me. "I'd like that. Besides, we can get to know each other better that way." When my brows rise, she continues. "Couples that can cook together tend to get along better. At least, that's what my grandma used to tell me."

I nod. This is good. She is already considering me as a potential mate. If this is how humans judge their mates, I will cook every meal with her so that she can assess our compatibility. I resolve to prove myself to her this afternoon.

CHAPTER 16

ANNA

This place is incredible. I can't believe he built a cabin with his bare hands. I follow him onto the second-floor deck and find that the view of the mountain forests is breathtaking. Dense forests full of green and purple trees and vegetation as far as the eye can see. I've never seen anything this incredible, even in the images I've seen of old Earth. "This is beautiful," I murmur. "How often do you come out here?"

"Not as much as I would like," he says. "Would you like a cup of tea before we begin our day?"

"Sure."

He brings me a round mug with no handle. I notice that none of the glasses or cups on this planet seem to have them. However, the material they're made of doesn't conduct heat, so it's never hot to the touch.

Varus likes to drink tea in the mornings as well. I've had a cup with him and Lilly out in the gardens a handful of times since we moved to Valoria. It's sweet with a slightly bitter undertone, but I've learned to enjoy it. The ritual reminds me of when I used to start my mornings with a warm cup of coffee.

I lift the mug to my face for a drink but stop when I don't recognize the scent. I place it on the small table and address Kaj. "What kind of tea is this?"

"A special blend that I created last season," he explains. "I believe it is the best one I've made so far."

I blink. "You make tea?"

"Yes. Every season I harvest the *valo* leaves then add different variations of dried fruits and flowers to create new and unique blends."

I smile. Now that I've seen all the work he put into building this house, it sounds like something he would do. As I study him, it occurs to me that he's exactly my type: thoughtful, introspective, intelligent. It doesn't hurt that he's irresistibly handsome, too. And those golden eyes—I could lose myself in their depths so easily.

"How did you get into blending teas?" I ask before taking a sip. Warm liquid coats my tongue in a burst of sweet citrus. "This is wonderful. So much better than that stuff Varus likes."

He laughs. "Yes, I've told him as much, but the bitter kind is his preference." He turns his gaze toward the forest, sadness flickering across his expression before he speaks. "I blame Varus for my tea obsession—as my sister used to call it." A wistful smile crests his lips. "He and his sister would visit us often. The four of us would sit on the larger balcony of the castle and drink tea together while we talked and played games."

His eyes are bright with tears, and I watch him blink them back. I reach across and gently place my hand over his. "You must miss her very much."

"I miss them both." His voice is thick with emotion. He

lifts his cup with a pained smile. "But this reminds me of the happy days we spent together."

I understand his pain. I lost my entire family to sickness on the ships. Jarod was all I had left and now... even he's gone. Sensing my sadness, Kaj turns his palm up to mine and gently squeezes. "I have upset you. Forgive me."

Despite my attempt to deny them, tears sting my eyes. "After I lost my family, one of the ship's doctors took me in. He treated me like his own daughter. We would drink coffee together every morning to start our day."

"What happened to him?" Kaj asks.

I close my eyes against the pain and swallow the lump in my throat. "He was killed by the pirates who attacked our ship. They shot him while we were running to the escape pods."

"My hearts grieve with yours," he whispers.

"Thank you."

I cast my gaze out to the forest as silence settles in the space between us. After a moment, I turn back to him. "I think Jarod would have liked it here. He was one of the oldest crewmembers. He always told me stories of his childhood and Earth-that-was before pollution overtook the planet."

Kaj nods. "We have recycling technologies here that should preserve our planet's ecosystem for many generations beyond ours."

"I'm glad. I was born on Earth after our people realized the land had been poisoned beyond saving. I don't remember anything but a dying planet. This place is like a paradise, Kaj."

Surveying the green and deep-purple trees, I am already in love with this world. I vow to do anything I can to protect it. And I can hardly wait to explore.

"I have always thought so, as well," he replies. "But then

again, I suppose each of the Clans thinks their territory the finest."

I shake my head. "I have not seen the Wind Clan lands yet, but I can't imagine they'd be more beautiful than this. This," I gesture to the forests and the mountains outside, "is everything I imagined for the new world we might find."

His expression seems to say, *This could be your home if you'd accept,* but he stays quiet.

I turn my eyes back toward the forest. "Where will you take me today?"

"I've heard that your people like surprises. So, I will not tell you."

"What?" My head snaps toward him and I frown. "Where did you hear this?"

"From Varus. He plans to surprise Lilliana on her birthing day with many gifts."

"Of course, he does." I laugh. "That man is a hopeless romantic."

"That he is," Kaj agrees. "Shall we be on our way?"

"Yes."

"First, you must dress warmly."

"Why?"

He lifts his gaze to the sky. "The wind. It has changed and will bring cooler air this day... possibly even rain."

I'm a bit impressed that he can predict the weather. "All I have is my dress," I tell him.

"I have robes here that you may use," he offers.

Eager to get going, I quickly dress in the robes he gave me. When I come back downstairs, he's waiting with another robe to layer on top. He carefully wraps it around me then cinches the waist to keep the fabric close to my body. I love the careful tenderness he lavishes on me—it makes me feel all warm inside.

"Ready?" He gives me a mischievous grin.

"Yes."

We follow a winding path from the cabin. I marvel at the vegetation growing along the way. I've never seen a forest so thick. Wide, gray trunks twist toward the sky, competing with their neighbors for a small patch of sunlight. They're covered in large heart-shaped leaves in deep green and small purple flowers. Bushes also line our way, overflowing with vibrant blue, yellow, and purple flowers like enormous roses.

He pulls one from the stem and offers it to me. I bring the soft petals to my nose, closing my eyes as I inhale the sweet fragrance. "This smells wonderful. It reminds me of roses on Earth."

"Yes, Varus has mentioned Lilliana likes them, as well." He pauses. "She told him that a gift of flowers is considered a romantic gesture. Part of the courtship ritual among humans." He picks a few more colorful flowers and hands them to me. "Is three an acceptable number or should I pick more?"

I laugh at his earnest expression. "Three is fine."

We walk a bit further and I ask again, "Where are we going?"

He arches a teasing brow. "I already told you, it is a surprise."

"Can you give me a hint?"

A crack of thunder booms overhead, startling me. I jump toward Kaj, and he wraps a protective arm around my waist, tugging me closer as he curls his wing around my form. His golden eyes meet mine as he strokes a soothing hand down my back. "You are safe."

I feel foolish for my sudden fear and feel the need to explain. After all, Drakarian females are fierce and brave, so I don't want him to think me weak. I don't know why, but his opinion is important to me. "It's been so long since we left Earth, I'd forgotten how loud storms can be."

"You are safe." He assures me again, tugging me even closer to his side. "But we should go back."

In his eyes, I see no judgment for my irrational fear. My insides heat. I feel I truly am safe with him. Safe to be unapologetically me. I think about his teasing promise and lament that our adventure will be cut short.

"But what about my surprise?"

His lips curl up in a faint smile. "It will have to wait until tomorrow."

We barely make it back to the cabin before the sky opens. I turn in the doorway and stare at the hard rain pelting the earth. The fresh scent of ozone and earth fills my nostrils as a dull roar echoes from the roof throughout the entire house. I listen in wonder. Cautiously, I reach out my hand, smiling when heavy droplets wet my skin.

"It's been so long since I've seen real rain," I whisper to myself, lost in reverie.

The light touch of Kaj's hand on my shoulder draws my attention, and I turn back to face him. "Would you like to sit on the balcony and watch the storm? I could make us some tea."

"That sounds lovely."

It doesn't take him long to warm two cups. We sit on the covered balcony and I enjoy the smell of the fresh rain. "When I was a kid, I used to love sitting outside on the porch with my dad, watching storms." I smile at the memory. "In the virtual reality rooms, the experience wasn't quite the same." Another crack of thunder sounds overhead, and I tense. I'd forgotten how intense a real storm can be.

The rain has brought a chill to the air, just as he suspected, and I shiver. He wraps his arm around me and I nestle into his side, sipping at my mug. My lips quirk up a fraction as he cautiously extends a wing and curls it around my shoulder.

"Is this all right?" he asks.

"Yes."

It truly is. At first, I was worried that Kaj would be too insistent. That he'd try to push himself on me or force me to accept the bond. But I love how carefully he ensures that I'm comfortable, always asking instead of taking as I'd feared.

He gives me a curious look. "Were you able to recreate all of your home planet's environments on the ship?"

"Just about." I look down at my hands, repressing the painful memory of all we lost during the attack. "I think those rooms are the only thing that kept us from going crazy. They made living on the ships all those years more bearable."

"It was wise of the builders to include them," he says. "Our vessels are built with similar technology for the same reason—to give the crew an escape if they need one."

I let out a wistful sigh as I stare out at the rain. "To think I used to spend my time in simulated mountain environments, dreaming about finding a mountainous world to settle on. And now... I'm finally here. In a place even more beautiful than anything I could have imagined."

"There is still so much more for you to see. Your people have an entire new world to explore."

I recline in my chair as I consider the possibilities. I take another sip of my tea, allowing the warm liquid to roll across my tongue to savor the delicate flavor. "I'd like to see the Wind Clan territory sometime. Skye says it's beautiful, composed of floating islands."

"It is truth," he replies. "I can take you there some day, if you wish."

My heart flutters in my chest at his lovely smile. It's a wonderful dream to imagine traveling the world together.

"That sounds nice," I tell him. When his eyes light up, I worry that I'm leading him on. After all, this vacation *is* a trial run of sorts for our relationship. To see if we're truly compatible.

My heart is telling me to just take the leap. To fall into his arms and let the rest work itself out. But my mind insists we're falling too fast, and I need to be careful before committing to a lifetime together. But as his gaze holds mine, I cannot deny the longing that fills me.

Staring deep into his golden eyes, I lean closer until his lips are almost touching mine. I hesitate a moment, and he does too. He's waiting to see what I'll do and he's letting me lead.

Gently, I press my lips to his and then smile against them. "Is this all right?" I whisper.

He nods and I wrap my arms around his neck. With his chest pressed to mine, the pounding of his hearts is like an insistent drum against me and when I kiss him again, they begin hammering.

I trace my tongue along the seam of his lips, and when he opens his mouth, I deepen our kiss.

He moans as my tongue strokes against his. He wraps his wings around me and pulls me into his lap. Holding tightly to me, he rolls his hips against mine. The feel of his stav pressing against the entrance to my core, through my clothing, is the most exquisite torture.

He rips his mouth from mine and his nostrils flare as he stares at me with a heated gaze. "I can scent your need, my beautiful Anna," he rasps.

I stare deep into his eyes as I take his hand and guide it down my body to my folds. My robe falls off my shoulder, baring me to his gaze.

His mouth drifts open as he stares down at me. "You are perfect," he breathes.

Cautiously, he retracts his claws and then dips one finger between my folds. His pupils are blown wide so that only a thin rim of gold is barely visible around the edges. "You are already ready for me, my mate," he growls low in arousal.

"Can we just touch for now?" I whisper.

He nods. "I will take anything you will give me, Anna, and no more."

My heart clenches and I crush my lips to his. He wraps his wings around me, pulling me even closer. A low moan escapes me as he drags his fingers through my slick heat and finds the small bundle of nerves at the apex.

"Right there," I breathe.

He concentrates his attention on the sensitive pearl of flesh. His gaze holds mine intensely as he carefully inserts one finger into my channel. I inhale sharply as he inserts another.

He begins a slow and steady rhythm as he pumps them into me, and I'm lost in sensation.

His stav is hard against my inner thigh and I reach between us to gently touch him.

He hisses between his teeth as liquid beads on the end and then rolls down his shaft.

His gaze burns into mine, full of desire as he continues to pump his fingers into me, dragging me closer to the edge of my climax. "Kaj, please," I breathe and I'm not even sure what I'm asking for.

I gather a bead of his precum on my fingers and then drag it across my abdomen, marking me with his scent. He growls low and then takes my hand and moves it between my slick folds, marking me there as well. "I long to fill you with my essence and claim you as mine. To give you my seed and seal you to me, Anna."

"I—" I start to tell him that I want this. That I want him. More than anything. But I hesitate. I'm not sure I'm ready to become his mate just yet.

Sensing my hesitation, he cups my cheek. "We will not fully mate until you decide," he vows.

I wrap my hand around his stav, surprised that my fingers do not quite touch because he is so large. The delicious ridges along his shaft drive my desire even higher as I imagine him filling me completely.

"Just touching for now," I whisper.

He growls low in arousal as I move against his hand. "I want only to give you pleasure, Anna."

My head falls back as he brushes his thumb over the sensitive pearl of flesh between my folds while moving his fingers back and forth deep inside me. He leans forward and closes his mouth over my breast, laving his tongue across the peak.

I moan as he begins a gentle suction. I thread my fingers through his hair and then trace them down his back. His entire form is covered in thick layers of muscle. I can feel the tension in his body as he holds himself back, trying so hard to be careful with me.

It only makes me want him that much more. "Kaj," I whisper against his skin as I press a soft kiss to his neck.

He quickens his pace and I close my eyes as heat pools deep in my core.

He cups my cheek, and I open my eyes to find him staring at me with a half-lidded gaze. "I want to watch you as you find your release, my beautiful Anna."

His words spark something deep inside me. Desire fills my entire body and then I'm coming harder than I ever have before. I cry out his name as wave after wave of pleasure rushes through me.

When I finally come down from my climax, I practically melt against him. My entire body goes limp in his arms. His golden gaze holds mine as he takes his fingers into his mouth to taste me. He closes his eyes and growls low in his throat as if I am the best thing he's ever had. "Your nectar is exquisite," he murmurs.

He drops his forehead to mine then curls his wings around me even tighter. "You are perfect, Anna."

I allow myself to drift away in his arms, knowing that I'm safe. That he'd never do anything I don't want.

When I wake, I don't know how long it's been that he's held me like this. I lift my head to his and he smiles down at me and presses a kiss to my forehead. "Are you hungry, my beautiful Anna?"

"Thirsty," I reply.

"Then, let us go downstairs," he murmurs.

I wrap my robe back around me, fastening it in place before I follow him down the stairs. I don't bathe because I remember Lilly telling me how important scent marking is to Drakarians. Besides, I kind of like the idea of being marked by my mate.

My mate. The words echo in my mind. The truth is... I'm already considering him to be mine. Even though I want to go slow and not rush into anything, I cannot deny how much I want him. How much I trust him and how much I want to be his in return.

I force myself to think of other things as I follow him into the kitchen. He said he'd show me how to use all the appliances, and I figure learning how to make tea is as good a place to start as any. I'm surprised when he opens one of the cabinets and I notice several clear glass containers of dried tea.

"Wow. You have quite the collection here." I feel silly for believing the blend Varus gave us was the only one available on this world.

He tilts his chin up a notch. "I've expanded my selection over the past few cycles. The last time I went off-world, I even brought back some herbs from Luralo station."

"How often do you go off world?"

"Not very often," he replies. "The only reason I do so is to attend important meetings of the Galactic Federation when they request attendance from the planets within the alliance. And they are always held on Luralo station. If you wish to go with me, I can—"

"No, thank you," I reply quickly. "I think I've had enough of space to last a lifetime."

"If you are worried about pirates, our ships are safe and heavily armored. The other races tend to leave us alone because they know we are fierce warriors."

"When do you have to go again?" I ask, considering his offer.

"Within the next few months."

A thought occurs to me. "Do the others go? Varus? Raidyn? Llyr?"

"No. That is why it is important that I attend the meetings on behalf of our world. My Clan has always been neutral—never taking sides in any wars between the others. The other Clans trust us—the Earth Clan—to represent them at the alliance meetings." He pauses. "And it is good this way because it makes us seem more united than we actually are."

I tip my head to the side to regard him. "That's a lot of responsibility on yours shoulders."

"Yes," he agrees. "It can be... stressful."

"Maybe now after the Summit, you can all take turns going to represent Drakaria. Now that everyone seems to be getting along."

He nods. "You are right. I will bring this up with the others. It is a good plan. You are very wise, Anna."

I blush at the compliment.

He turns his attention back to the various tea blends and pulls down a glass jar, "This is my favorite blend so far."

"Can I try some?"

"Of course. I believe you will enjoy it."

He places the dried leaves in a small metal strainer like the ones we used on the ships and shows me how to boil the water. He arches a brow. "Did you not have appliances in your apartment in Valoria?"

"We did, but they were different from what you seem to have here. We relied pretty heavily on the stasis unit and warmer to keep and prepare our meals. I never cooked anything there." My eyes sweep over the kitchen. "I'm getting hungry. Can we make dinner a bit early?"

He nods. "Let's start with something simple, and then we'll move on to more complex dishes as you learn."

A smirk twists my lips. He sounds confident that I'm going to be around him long enough to become a gourmet chef. To be honest, I like the idea. As we go through the meal prep for a dish that reminds me of spaghetti, I find myself smiling more than I have in a long time.

We chat while we finish adding all the ingredients then place the dish in the warmer to finish cooking. "What about dessert?" I tease.

He arches a brow. "Dessert is much easier to prepare, but should not be eaten before the main meal."

I remember my mom giving the same advice. I guess some customs are universal. "I agree. So, what did you have in mind?"

A grin splits his face. "I believe you will enjoy coliza."

I hum in acknowledgment. "I've never heard of it, but I trust you."

His smile grows even brighter, baring two rows of sharp fangs. Instead of scaring me, the sight only makes me appreciate how carefully and patiently he treats me. This man is an apex predator on this world, yet he's so gentle and caring when it comes to me and my comfort.

When the coliza is ready, I realize we've made the

Drakarian version of chocolate chip cookies. However, I'm hesitant to try them because I don't want to be disappointed.

He offers me the first one.

Cautiously, I take a small bite. A burst of a taste eerily similar to dark chocolate floods my tongue. I close my eyes and hum in pleasure. I never thought I'd taste this again.

CHAPTER 17

KAJ

She takes a small bite of coliza and closes her eyes. A sensual hum sounds in the back of her throat, close to the soft moans she made earlier when we were touching. It makes me want to pull her into my arms and capture her mouth with my own. I want to bear her to the ground and taste her sweet nectar on my tongue again as I did earlier.

I want to sheathe myself deep inside her and fill her with my essence, claiming her as my mate.

Swallowing thickly, I force myself to remain still. She does not want to fully mate yet. I must wait for her to make the first move. Though it is difficult, the reward is worth the wait. Normally, I am a patient male. But when she takes another bite of her coliza and a crumb sticks to the edge of her lower lip, I must curl my fingers into my palms as a distraction from the urge to pull her into my arms and seal my mouth over hers.

"Kaj?" She stares up at me curiously.

"Yes?"

"Are you all right?"

I mean to reassure her, but instead, I say, "I'm uncertain."

Her small brow furrows. "What's wrong?"

I clear my throat, turning my attention back to our meal. "The food should be thoroughly cooked if you'd like to check on the warmer now."

She studies me for another moment before turning to the warmer. A smile lights her face when she pulls out our dinner and sets it on the counter. "Ta-da!"

I cock my head to the side. "This is... not translating correctly."

"It just means you should be impressed with my cooking skills," she teases.

"You are a fast learner. I already am impressed by everything you do." I grin.

I'm rewarded with another of her dazzling smiles. She is perfect, my mate. Now, if only I could convince her to be mine.

We take our food to the balcony and watch the rain fall endlessly outside. She takes in the world around her in such wonder. "It must have been difficult living on a ship for so many cycles."

Sadness flits across her expression. "It was. That's why I always tried to keep busy with work. It made the days seem to pass by quicker."

I lean forward. "What made you decide to become a healer?"

"When I was little, I got sick with a virus. I couldn't even get out of bed because I was so weak. The doctor—Healer, I mean," she corrects. "She stayed with me, even though I put her at risk of infection. She never gave up on me, and slowly, I got better." She pauses. "I remember thinking that I wanted to be able to do that someday. It wasn't just that she healed me; she sat with me, made me laugh... we even played a few games. She didn't just take care of me, she brought me joy." She lifts her gaze to mine. "Does that make sense?"

"Yes."

"What about you?" she asks. "What made you become a Healer?"

"My grandfather was a Healer. I used to follow him everywhere, even to work." I smile at the distant memory. "Seeing what he was able to do for the ill was inspiring. He was my hero, I suppose. Eventually, he became my teacher and my mentor."

"Where is he now?"

I lower my gaze to my hands, remembering how I tried so hard to save my family. "He died when the plague swept through our world. He and my sister, only a few days apart."

"I'm sorry." She places a hand atop mine. "That must have been devastating."

Clenching my jaw, I struggle to push down the pain. "I've carried the guilt of their passing for a long time."

"And now?"

I lift my eyes to hers. "I understand that there are some things only the gods can decide, despite the plans that we may make."

She nods. "I learned that lesson, too. Watching my parents and so many of our crew die when the flu went through the ships, I... I felt so useless."

I turn my palm up to hers and gently squeeze her hand as her gaze holds mine. "It is hard for a Healer to watch a patient cross from this world to the next. I believe it is because we are taught how to keep people alive, so when we fail, letting them go is like going against all we have ingrained in ourselves."

Moisture gathers in the corners of her eyes. "Yes. It is." She sniffs. "I'm sorry, I... shouldn't be so emotional."

The first tear escapes her lashes and rolls down her cheek. I reach across and brush it away with the pad of my thumb. "There is no shame in grieving the ones whom we have lost. Ever."

A faint smile crests her lips. "Thank you, Kaj."

I wish I could take away her pain. I understand now why she is so strong, my linaya. She has lost everything—her entire family—and yet, she is a survivor, forging a new life in a strange world.

I think of the first time I met her; how skillfully she treated her patients even though she'd only recently begun her training. I marvel at her tenacity and intelligence, and I pray to the gods that she will desire me as hers—fully. I can think of no other I would ever want as my mate. Anna is perfect. We understand one another, and it is so easy to share things with her that I've kept to myself all these cycles.

The rain picks up, and she turns her gaze to the forest with a small sigh. "It's so peaceful here, Kaj. I could sit on this balcony for days just enjoying this view."

I am pleased that she likes my nest. After all, I built this place intending to impress my future mate. "We can stay as long as you wish."

She turns back to me. "You said you used to play games with Varus. What kind of games?"

I hoped she would ask. It has been a long time since I've had a partner to play with. "Narku," I tell her. "It is a game of chance and strategy."

"How so?"

"One moment." I lift my hand to indicate she should wait. "I will return with the game shortly."

It doesn't take me long to find the dusty box in the closet. When I return, I lay all the pieces out on the table and arrange them in their proper starting layout.

She studies the board as I explain the rules, biting her

lower lip as if in deep concentration. I cannot tell from her expression if she finds my description confusing, so I ask, "What do you think?"

"It reminds me of chess, a human game I love."

"Chess," I repeat the word, committing it to memory. "Explain it to me and I shall have a board made so that you may teach me how to play."

"You want to learn?" Her eyes are sparkling with barely contained joy.

When she regards me so sweetly, I am tempted to learn anything she wishes. "Yes."

"All right." She smiles. "Teach me how to play this. We can move on to chess later."

Happiness blooms in my chest. She is already making plans with me, something she was hesitant to do only a short while earlier. This is good. I hope that means she enjoys our time together as much as I do.

As we play, she describes in great detail the human game of chess. She even draws several images on my tablet to explain what each piece can do. I make several notes so that I may recreate this for her later.

The sun drops low on the horizon, painting the mountainous landscape in vivid shades of yellow, orange, and red. I retrieve another coliza for her from the kitchen, surprised and pleased in equal measure by her healthy appetite.

When it is time to sleep, she takes a bath in the cleansing room while I prepare a bed for myself on the couch downstairs. She has not yet indicated that she wishes to touch or mate me, so I will make certain she does not feel pressured to share a bed with me.

I take my turn in the bathing pool after her, taking extra care to scrub my scales clean. When I look in the mirror, I smile to myself. They are practically glowing. Surely, she will be impressed.

I step out of the cleansing room, discreetly flexing my biceps as I walk into the bedroom, hoping she will notice me. To my disappointment, she is already asleep in bed. Quietly, I move to her side and gently tuck the blanket around her shoulders to make sure she is warm.

I study her as she sleeps. She and her kind are so much smaller than Drakarian females. Asleep like this, she appears so vulnerable, so fragile, that the sight breaks me. I wonder if this is how Varus and Raidyn feel. Are they constantly worried about the safety of their mates?

With blunted claws and flat, white teeth, I wonder how her race managed to survive as a species. They do not even have wings. They have evolved no natural defenses to speak of—the thought alone terrifies me.

I hope the humans never ask us to take them back into space. Her people are beautiful; many alien races would prey upon them. I shudder inwardly as I think of how many humans went missing after the pirates attacked their ship. I hope they were able to find some semblance of safety.

My people have sent out ships to search for other survivors, but thus far, we have found nothing on the planet or in space.

With a final glance at my mate, I move downstairs and take my place on the couch. It is not as comfortable as the bed, but it will do.

CHAPTER 18

ANNA

Edward's eyes flash with anger as he backs me against the wall. "You can't just break up with me. We haven't even gotten to the good parts of the relationship."

"I—I'm sorry." I'm so scared at the way he's acting that I stumble over my words. "It's just not working out. And I—"

He hits my face with the back of his hand. My head is spinning while he cages me in his arms. I fight against his hold. "No!"

"Anna! Wake up!" a deep voice calls above me.

My eyes snap open to find Kaj kneeling beside the bed, his expression full of concern. The raw pain of my nightmare is still fresh. Tears spill down my face as I struggle to contain it. I throw my arms around him, burying my face in his chest as great, hiccupping sobs rack my body.

He climbs into bed and tugs me against him, wrapping his arms and wings around me as he soothingly runs his hand up and down my back. He whispers in my ear, "It is all right. You were having a nightmare. You are safe now. My vow."

"He tried to rape me." My voice quavers. "I was so scared.

I blamed myself for so long. If I hadn't opened the door to him. If I had just..." My voice trails off. I've been through this so many times before. All the what-ifs.

"It is not your fault," he murmurs, combing my hair between his fingers. "No male should ever force himself upon a female." His golden eyes stare deep into mine, full of concern. "I vow that I will always protect you, Anna. I will die before I ever let anyone harm you." He takes my hand and places it over his fate mark. "Even if you never choose me, Anna, I will always make sure you are safe."

His gaze holds mine and I know this is true. He would die to protect me. His arms and wings form a warm embrace around me. When was the last time someone made me feel so safe?

I open my mouth to speak, but the words won't come. Emotions lodge in my throat, and I rest my head against his shoulder as I allow my tears to fall unchecked.

"I thought he was a good guy. We'd known each other for years." A broken sob escapes me. "After he tried to rape me, he convinced me it wasn't his fault. He blamed his behavior on alcohol. I wanted so badly to believe him, so I let it go. But then, another girl came into the clinic." I shake my head, full of regret. "He tried to do the same to her, and I was so angry at myself for letting him hurt another that I..." Drawing in a deep breath, I give Kaj the truth I've never told anyone else before. "I killed him, Kaj."

I search his expression for any sign of shock or horror, but see none.

I continue. "His new victim told me she'd gotten away from him by sealing him in the airlock. So, I went to find him."

"What happened?"

"When I reached the door to the airlock, we were alone." I pause as the memory comes rushing back. "I asked him what he'd done—got him to admit that he'd tried to rape her. I told him he disgusted me. He got mad, claiming she'd asked for it, just like he said I had. It made me so angry. I never asked to be assaulted. I was so full of rage over what he'd done that I slammed my hand on the panel and spaced him. Everyone thought he died in an accident. I've never told another soul what I did." Hesitantly, I admit the dark truth I've carried since that day. "I don't regret it, Kaj. And I would do it again if faced with the same choice."

Kaj's gaze holds mine as he places two fingers under my chin and then cups my face. "I am honored that you trust me with your truth. You did what you felt was right. You are strong and you are brave. He will never hurt anyone else because of you."

My heart feels lighter than it has in a long time. The dark secret I've held inside me these past few years was a constant weight that has finally been lifted. I rest my forehead against his and close my eyes. "Thank you for listening, Kaj," I whisper. "Thank you for understanding and not judging me."

"I will always listen." He gently brushes the hair back from my face, tucking it behind my ear in a tender gesture. "And I am sorry for what you went through, but it was not your fault what that male did to you." He pauses. "It took me a long time to realize that not everything is in my control. No matter how much I wish it to be."

"What about the bond?" I ask, confused by his confession. "Does it bother you that you cannot control whom the gods chose for you?"

All this time, I've just been thinking of myself. I never even stopped to consider that he might not have wanted the bond, either. It was thrust upon him and he feels he must accept it because his people believe it is the will of the gods. What if he doesn't want me? In fact, why should he? Here I've been pushing him away, when all the while, he's probably wondered why the gods would curse him with a mate who didn't even care enough to try until now.

All my doubts well up until I feel as if I'm drowning in anxiety. Of course, he wouldn't want me. I'm human, nothing like a Drakarian woman.

His reflective golden eyes meet mine, grounding me. He runs his hand over my hair. "I was attracted to you from the first moment we met. I knew even then that I desired you as mine. I've never experienced such joy as I did the moment the mark appeared for you. I have thanked the gods every day since for choosing you to be my linaya." He pauses and licks his lips nervously. "I only hope to become worthy of you. So that you will claim me as yours."

My heart clenches at his words. This man truly loves me for me—not because of some bond. Why am I fighting this? Would it be so bad to be his?

I reach up and cup his cheek. He leans into my palm as if relishing the touch of my skin against his. "I'm sorry, Kaj."

He frowns. "For what?"

"For pushing you away. I was so scared of messing up and falling so quickly because I thought it was all happening too fast. If not for my past, I wouldn't have held onto so much doubt. I trust you, Kaj."

He smiles. "It is all right, Anna. I am honored by your trust. We will not rush into anything. We have time to get to know one another better—for you to decide if you want me. I will not leave unless you ask me to. I am already yours, my linaya. I will wait for as long as you need to decide if you wish to be mine."

If I thought I was falling for him before, my heart is practically melting after those words. I brush the pad of my thumb across his soft, warm lips. This gorgeous man wants me. How did I get so lucky?

That's it. I've decided I'm not going to be afraid anymore.

If Kaj will wait until I'm ready, I'm all in. I'm going to give our relationship a chance—without holding back anymore.

"Kaj?"

"Yes?"

"Stay here with me tonight." I gesture for him to lie down. "We don't have to do anything. I just... want you to hold me while we sleep." My cheeks heat in embarrassment. "I want to be close to you. I love being wrapped in your arms and wings."

He gives me a smile as bright as the sun. "I will gladly hold you."

We lie down side by side and he tugs me against him. He curls his body protectively around mine and wraps his arm around my waist. His wings envelop both of us, and I snuggle closer, loving this intimacy between us.

He drops his forehead gently to mine and whispers, "Rest, my linaya. I have you."

Kaj makes me feel safe, something I haven't felt in a long time. I close my eyes and allow myself to drift away. Somehow, for the first time in what feels like forever, I know that I'll finally be able to sleep without nightmares.

CHAPTER 19

ANNA

When I wake up, the morning is no different from each morning past, except that I don't feel worried or afraid anymore. I'm wrapped up in Kaj's arms and wings, and I love how warm and protected that makes me feel. I turn in his arms to face him. "Good morning."

He gives me a sleepy smile. "Did you sleep well?"

"Yes. You?" Almost in answer, I feel his *stav* like a hard bar against my abdomen.

"Yes." He leans in and nudges my nose gently with his in such a sweet gesture that my heart melts and I can't stop smiling. "I will prepare a morning meal for you, my linaya."

I want to protest that I should help because I'd like to learn how to cook for myself. I open my mouth to speak, but he stands from the bed then glances over his shoulder. "Would you like to help?"

"Yes."

"Then I will meet you downstairs."

It doesn't take me long to get ready and join him in the kitchen. I open the tea cupboard and glance at his selection. Suddenly, I feel his presence behind me. His body radiates heat as he practically towers over me. He reaches for one of the many jars and hands it to me. "This one is preferable for a morning blend. I believe you will enjoy it," he boasts.

I boil the water and add the crushed leaves to steep while we start making breakfast. I'm surprised by how well we work together in near-perfect synchronization as we trade off various tasks. Once we've put all the ingredients together, I place the dish in the Drakarian version of an oven and watch in amazement as it cooks in only a few minutes.

"Shall we eat on the balcony?"

"That sounds perfect."

Breakfast tastes amazing, but I worry that he doesn't like my cooking because I notice he barely eats any. "Does it... taste all right?"

He nods. "It is delicious."

I point to his plate. "But you didn't eat much."

He tips his head to the side. "Drakarians do not require sustenance as often as humans."

A short puff of air escapes my lips as I laugh. "Of course." I roll my eyes in mock frustration. "As a doctor now studying Drakarians, you'd think I would have remembered that fact."

He smiles, seeming to understand. "Do not be so hard on yourself. You have not been here very long, and this world is entirely new to you. There is much I still do not know about your species, and I will need your help—all of our Healers will—so that we can learn to treat any human ailments."

He's right. Now that I think about it, they don't know much about us. For instance, Healer Ranas seriously believed that humans lay eggs. He asked Lilly how long it normally takes us to lay eggs after conception. At first, she was shocked, but now we joke about his mistake frequently.

I take a sip of my tea and a sweet flavor bursts across my tongue. My eyes snap toward Kaj. "This blend is even better than the one we had last night."

"I am pleased you like it." He grins. "I used some of the lotae flowers in this one. They add a hint of sweetness to this mixture."

"That's amazing, Kaj. How do you know what to blend?"

He tips his head to the side as if considering before he answers. "We of the Earth Clan are connected to all life on this planet, even more so than those of the other Clans. Our kind can sense the"—his brows pinch together as if he's struggling to find the right word before finally settling on —"life force of each plant. The journey it has taken from seed to maturity."

"That's amazing." I knew each of the Clans was named after an element, but I did not realize they had a deeper connection to the element they embody. "I knew your people could breathe different types of fire, but I didn't know your abilities were further connected to nature."

"Only the Earth Clan is."

"Why is that?"

"We do not know." He pauses. "However, as a result, many of our people are farmers. They can gauge the health of their land and grow crops without depleting the soil of vital nutrients."

"That's amazing." I didn't know a species could be so in tune with their world. If only humans had shared a similar connection with Earth, perhaps we wouldn't have polluted our planet past the point of saving. I wonder what more there is to learn about Drakaria.

Which reminds me...

"Are you going to show me my surprise today?"

He smiles and reaches his hand toward mine. I take it without question. "Let us go."

~

We walk the same path we took yesterday, though the rain has softened the ground and made each step difficult. Patches of mud suck at my shoes slowing our progress. Kaj turns to me. "I can carry you, if you'd like. Or we could even fly."

I deliberate for a moment. "Let's fly."

He steps forward. One hand slides behind my back and the other below my knees, then he lifts me off my feet. I yelp in surprise before he tucks me into his chest. "I did not expect that," I laugh. "I thought you were going to shift."

"No. This form allows me to see you while we are in flight, and I would prefer to witness the look on your face when we reach our destination."

Well, he's certainly building this surprise up. Now I'm imagining all sorts of wonders. It's even more exciting than opening presents on my birthday. "Can you give me a hint?" I bat my eyelashes at him teasingly.

He laughs. "No. You cannot persuade me to ruin the surprise, even if you use all of your charms and beauty."

"Fine," I pretend to pout. "I'll just have to wait and see."

"Yes." He smirks. "You will."

Without warning, he jumps and lifts into the sky. His wings billow like great sails as he catches the wind and we ascend even higher. From here, I can see the house at the end of the path. It's more isolated than I realized, but that only adds to its charm. It's like our own private, hidden getaway, and I love it.

My face heats as Kaj's strong arms flex around me. He scans the skies, searching for danger. His strong jaw is set in an almost stern expression. He really is a handsome man.

Even as I think this, I wonder when I stopped considering him an alien. Though he has wings and scales and a tail and more, to me... he's simply Kaj. A faint smile ghosts across my lips.

"What is it?" He searches my face.

"Nothing. I was just thinking about this world and... you." I mutter the last word in a voice so low I wonder if he's even heard me.

"What about me?" he asks, and I realize he has much better hearing than I thought. He grins. "Are you thinking about how handsome I am and what an excellent mate I would be?"

His eyes sparkle with barely contained amusement as he waits for my answer. I would laugh, but the truth is that he *is* all those things. I twine my arms tightly around his neck and rest my head against his chest. "Yes," I admit. "All the good things about you."

He gently nuzzles the top of my head and my heart flutters at just that small touch. I'm falling so hard for this man.

The canopy is so thick it's difficult to see the ground. A dull roar up ahead draws my attention, and when I lift my head, I stare in wonder at a beautiful waterfall.

Crystal-clear water cascades from a mountain above before dropping into a large pool at the base. Kaj circles overhead for a moment before gently setting us down.

"Is this my surprise?"

He sets my feet on the ground, looking earnest. "Yes. Does it please you?"

"It's beautiful."

He takes my hand then leads me to the water's edge. "Although the water comes from the mountains, a warm spring lies beneath this pool. It heats the water, but not unbearably so," he adds. "I thought you might like to take a swim."

I love that idea. How many times did I swim in the virtual reality room on the ship, wishing the water were real?

I take a step back to disrobe, leaving only my underwear on.

Kaj's jaw drops and his brows fly up. "I—I thought your people did not like nudity."

I laugh. "This," I gesture to myself, "is close enough to a swimsuit. Besides," I shrug, "as long as the important parts are covered, I'm not nude."

He puts his hand to his chin, lifting thoughtful eyes to the sky. "Interesting. I will keep this in mind."

I wade into the water. Just like he said, it's warm, inviting, and oh-so-relaxing. With a soft sigh of contentment, I tip to float on my back, staring up at the sky. A rippling wave disturbs the pool's surface, and I glance to the side to find Kaj wading toward me.

When he reaches my side, I take his hand in mine and pull myself to him. He hooks his arms under my back and knees, holding me close while I float. I rest my head against his chest. "This is perfect."

"Yes. It is one of my favorite places," he replies. "I come here as often as I can."

A small fish swims past us, followed quickly by another flash of bright blue and yellow. "What are those called?" I point at them.

"Zatari," he replies. "They can live in both fresh and saltwater."

A bright-orange fish zips past as I peer at the bottom of the pool. It's amazing how clear the water is—I can see every pebble on the ground. "Want to swim with me?" I ask.

His golden eyes meet mine, full of promise. "I would love to."

We swim across the pool, and I decide to dive under the water, taking in my surroundings in wide-eyed wonder as small fish flit by my head. When I emerge, Kaj is nowhere to be found, but I figure he's probably just diving like I was only a moment ago.

I wait and wait for him to surface. I scan the water for any sign of him but see nothing. Now I'm starting to worry. What if he drowned?

Frantic, I dive back under, searching for him. He shouldn't be hard to find given that he's enormous compared to the fish—and green. Almost instantly, I spot him. His head turns toward me, and he begins swimming my way, his tail cutting through the water to provide forward momentum. When he reaches me, we both break through the surface.

I throw my arms around his neck. I can't help it. I was so worried when I thought something had happened to him. "You were under a long time," I tell him. "How long can you hold your breath?"

He pulls back, head tilted. "I did not hold my breath. I was breathing underwater."

"You can breathe underwater?" I blurt. "That's amazing."

His tail wraps around my waist and drags me closer. He holds me to his chest as his golden eyes meet mine. "I did not realize your species could not. Now I am rethinking the wisdom of us remaining in the water. I do not want you to drown."

I roll my eyes. "I know how to swim. I'm not going to drown, Kaj."

He sighs heavily. "Forgive me. I know Drakarian females do not like an overly protective male, but I cannot help but worry for your safety." He lifts my hand and stares down at my fingers, probably thinking about the fact that humans don't have claws. "Your species has no natural defenses. It is... concerning," he adds in a low voice.

Even though I should be offended since Drakarians are almost constantly making remarks about how helpless and fragile they think we are, I'm not. When he tugs me closer to his chest and holds me like I'm the most precious treasure in the world, warmth blooms in my chest. I feel so loved and protected that I can't complain. When was the last time someone took care of me?

Since Jarod died, no one has. Not until Kaj.

I lift my chin to look up at him. His eyes meet mine, promising a lifetime of love. I twine my arms around his neck, and he crouches in the water until his face is even with mine. I lean in to press my lips to his.

He opens his mouth and curls his tongue around mine. I moan against his lips because his ridged tongue feels so amazing. He tastes like cinnamon and spice, and I can't get enough of him.

I wrap my legs around his waist and pull myself even closer to his body. So close that no space is left between us anymore. His *stav* is hard against my inner thigh.

His tail winds around my leg as his hold tightens. With one arm banded around my back to hold me in place, he runs the other down the length of my body.

I moan into his mouth as he cups my breast through the fabric of my bra. I want him to touch me, so I reach up and unhook the clasp. "Touch me," I whisper against his lips. "I want your hands on me."

He kisses a heated trail down my neck to the curve of my shoulder. He brushes his thumb across my breast, and my nipple hardens to a beaded tip beneath his attentions. It feels so good, I roll my hips against his, and he groans as his *stav* lines up with my folds. Only the thin fabric of my underwear separates him from my entrance.

I want him so badly, but I know his people mate for life. Once we seal the bond, there is no going back. He will be mine, and I will be his.

As if sensing my hesitation, he pulls back and rests his

forehead against mine. "May I taste you, my beautiful linaya? We do not have to fully mate until you are ready."

I know he said he loves the way I taste, but I'm still surprised by this. I always thought men didn't enjoy that. At least, that's what I've heard about human men. "Are you... sure?" I hedge.

His golden eyes burn with passion. "I have dreamed of tasting your sweet nectar again. Please, allow me to pleasure you with my tongue, Anna."

I blink in astonishment. How can I deny him when he asks me like this? His rough tone sparks desire deep in my core. "Yes," I reply, breathless with anticipation. Yesterday, he used his fingers, but today he wants to use his tongue. I've never done this before. Although I'm slightly nervous, I don't hesitate because it's Kaj. He loves me. If I get uncomfortable or want him to stop for any reason, he will.

I unwrap my legs from his waist so we can move to the shore, but he surprises me by sinking beneath the water. His lips leave small, suctioning kisses from my neck down to the valley of my breasts. It feels so amazing, I run my fingers through his hair, holding him to me.

When he closes his mouth over my breast, I tug at his hair and a low moan escapes me.

My heart beats wildly in my chest as he alternates between a soft scrape of his teeth and a gentle suction. The combination drives me mad with desire. He turns his attention to the other breast, and I wrap my legs around him again.

He continues down my body until he reaches my mons. His fingers slip beneath the fabric of my underwear and slide them off my hips, leaving me completely bare before him.

He dips his ridged tongue between my folds and immediately finds the small bundle of nerves at the top. I arch against him, wanting more. Digging my hands deeper into his hair, I hold him in place.

Lilly said that Varus was surprised when he discovered her clit because Drakarian women don't have one. But Kaj teases mine expertly with his tongue, making me suspect he learned this trade secret from his friend. If they are sharing tips, I'm not about to complain, because it feels incredible.

When he moves away from the sensitive pearl of flesh, I only have a moment to be disappointed before he dips his tongue into my core. The ridges dragging along the inside of my channel make me gasp and moan in pleasure.

I've touched myself before, but it never felt like this. Now that his tongue is inside me, I'm imagining how delicious his ridged *stav* will feel when we make love.

He replaces his tongue with his finger. He teases and lightly grazes his teeth across the softly hooded flesh of my folds, driving my desire even higher. When he applies a soft suction, I cry out and arch against him, tipping over the edge. Wave after wave washes through me as I orgasm harder than I ever have before.

He moves back up my body. Emerging from the water, he wraps his tail around my waist and his arms around my back as he drops his forehead to mine.

"You taste incredible, Anna," he whispers. He presses his lips to mine in a tender kiss as a low growl rumbles his chest. His *stav* is still hard against my abdomen.

"Do you want me to touch you?" I reach between us and wrap my hand around his length.

The breath hisses from his lungs as I gently stroke him. His tail wraps around my wrist, pulling me away. He clenches his jaw and stares down at me with hunger burning in his gaze. "I desire your touch more than anything else, but I want the first time I release to be deep inside you."

My thighs involuntarily clench at his words. I imagine

him moving over me, stroking long and deep inside my channel. At this moment, I'm ready to tell him that I want him now. I want everything. I want him to claim me and make love to me under the open sky. I brush my fingers across his cheek as I stare deep into his golden eyes.

Something screeches in the distance and Kaj stills. A booming roar follows, and my heart begins hammering in my chest. I hug him close to me. "What is that?"

"A lukota," he replies. "A predator."

I inhale sharply, but he cups my face and rubs my cheek with his thumb as if to soothe me.

"Do not fear. It is no match for me if it dares to attack. I will protect you. My vow."

And just like that, my fear dissolves.

A crash of leaves in the brush draws our attention as two creatures fly from the canopy, one chasing the other. The prey is scaled in orange-and-white strips and orange butterfly-like wings. If I had to describe the animal, I would say it looked like a cross between a bobcat and a dragon.

The predator looks like a hybrid between a wolf and a flying snake, with gnashing fangs and obsidian scales. Its red eyes fall on Kaj and it quickly retreats into the forest.

I watch as the cat-dragon struggles to remain aloft before crashing to the sand near the water. The poor creature is so cute and pitiful, my first instinct is to help. But I don't want to be stupid, so I ask Kaj, "Is this one dangerous?"

"Only when threatened."

As if he knows we're talking about him, the injured cat-dragon lifts his head with a mewl. My heart breaks. "Oh, Kaj. We need to help."

"Camali are wild creatures. This one may not allow you to help," he warns. "We should approach with caution."

"I have to try."

Determined, I wade back to shore and cover myself with

145

my robe before moving closer to the camali. Kaj is right behind me, and as we approach, I notice that one of the animal's wings is bent at an odd angle. As if to demonstrate the injury is serious, he flaps helplessly then releases a whimper of pain.

I look back at Kaj. "Do you think we can fix the wing?"

His eyes are glued on the camali as he nods affirmatively.

I reach out very slowly, holding my flattened palm as close as I dare to his nose, allowing him to sniff me.

His cat-like green-rimmed pupils expand as he watches me. His nostrils flare to scent my hand. The camali opens his mouth to release another whimper and my eyes go wide when I spot a row of gleaming white fangs.

This thing may look like a cat from Earth, but I've never seen a cat with teeth that sharp and deadly before. Despite my fear, I keep my hand as steady as possible, not wanting to startle the animal.

After a moment, he lowers his head to the sand as if in defeat. His injuries must be so severe that he has given up. Kaj moves closer as I gently stroke my hand over his scaled body, surprised to find him soft and smooth instead of rough. A purr vibrates his chest.

"The camali knows we mean no harm," Kaj says. "No animal would be purring otherwise."

Tears sting my eyes, but I blink them back as I pet the poor camali. "How can we help, Kaj? What should we do?"

Kaj lays his hand next to mine on the animal's back. He gently props up the broken wing with his other, leaning forward to breathe his healing flame over the break.

At first, the camali's eyes grow wide with alarm, but he must realize eventually that Kaj is helping because I see his muscles relax. His eyelids flutter as he lays his head down and falls asleep.

I turn to Kaj. "We should take him back to the house with us. We can't leave him here while he's vulnerable."

He nods. "I agree."

Kaj scoops the camali up into his arms and then hands him to me. Carefully, I cradle him to my chest, tenderly running my hand over his scales to pet him.

"We will have to fly back."

Kaj picks me up and holds me tightly as he lifts off.

It doesn't take long to reach the house. Once we do, Kaj sets about making a small bed for the creature in the corner of the living area downstairs.

"Camali make nests," he tells me as he fluffs two blankets together. "Hopefully, this one will be satisfied."

CHAPTER 20

KAJ

My mate has such a tender heart. I finish making the creature's temporary nest for recovery. When I turn back to Anna, I find her cradling the camali to her chest. Gently, she runs her hands over the scales as she coos lovingly.

"You're going to be all right, angel. Yes, you are," she murmurs. "Kaj is making you a nice, fluffy bed to sleep in."

A smile tugs at my lips. If she cares so deeply for a camali, I am certain she will be an excellent mother to our fledglings.

She walks over to me. "What should we name him?"

"This camali is female." I grin.

"Oh." She chuckles. "Then how about 'Callie?'"

I arch a brow. "Is it a human custom to name creatures you rescue?"

She laughs again and shrugs. "Kind of. My grandparents once rescued a tabby cat named Callie after she was attacked by another animal. This camali reminds me of her."

I glance down at the small predator. "Callie," I repeat the name as I gently stroke her head.

Although she is still unconscious, the camali instinctively flexes her paw around two of Anna's fingers, revealing several long, dark claws. Despite the lethal talons, Anna coos again then looks at me. "Maybe we should let her sleep with us."

My mate is brave. "Although camali are only dangerous when threatened, I would not think it wise to bring one to the bed," I gently caution. "She will be fine down here."

Anna sighs and carefully places Callie in her makeshift nest.

A sharp pain stabs at the center of my chest as I turn to my linaya. She allowed me to pleasure her, but she still has yet to accept me as her mate. Memories of our time by the waterfall float through my mind.

I want to claim her and fill her with my essence. To release inside her until my seed takes root deep in her womb, filling her with my child. I want every male who sees her to know she is mine and mine alone. None may ever touch her but me. I desire no other female by my side.

However, if I want a future with my linaya, I must convince her that I will be a good mate.

I curl my fingers reflexively into my palm, remembering the feel of her petal-soft skin. I long to touch her again. I want to pleasure her beneath the stars until she cries out my name as she finds her release.

But I must wait for her to approach me. She trusted me with her secret, and I realize that she must be the one in control so that she feels safe after all she has been through.

Anna breaks through my thoughts. "Should we start dinner?"

She loved the *cookies*, as she called them earlier, so we make another batch for dessert. When dinner is ready, she checks on the sleeping camali one last time before we head onto the balcony to eat.

When we are finished, she curls up on the bench beside me. I wrap an arm and wing around her, hugging her close to my side.

She releases a small sigh of contentment as she snuggles into me. "I love this," she says. "Just being here with you like this. It makes me feel happy and... safe."

My chest fills with pride that my mate is so pleased to be with me. Her trust is a gift that I vow to cherish and never break.

"I enjoy spending time with you as well, Anna."

She lifts her gaze to mine. "Kaj, I... wanted to tell you something earlier today... at the waterfall."

I tip my head to the side to regard her. "What is it?"

"I love you," she whispers. "And I trust you. I know you would never hurt me." She lowers her gaze. "I'm sorry I pushed you away in the beginning."

My hearts soar as happiness blooms in my chest. I place two fingers up under her chin and tip her face up to mine as I stare deep into her beautiful green eyes. "I love you too, Anna."

A stunning smile curves her mouth. She cups her hand to the back of my neck and pulls my lips down to hers. I open my mouth and deepen our kiss as she pulls herself into my lap.

She wraps her legs and arms around me, and I fold my wings over her. "Will you be mine, Anna?" I ask between kisses. "Will you accept me as your mate?"

She dips her hands beneath the collar of my robe and slides it back from my shoulders. Her heated gaze holds mine as she removes hers as well. "I want you, Kaj. I want to be yours."

Her scent is intoxicating, driving me mad with desire. I

flare my nostrils and draw in a deep breath, inhaling her delicate, heady fragrance.

My stav presses insistently against the inside of my mating pouch, seeking her warm entrance. Gritting my teeth, I will my body to relax, but it is no use. I long to bury myself deep inside her.

She squeaks as I wrap my arms and wings tightly around her, pulling her close so that there is no space between us. She opens her mouth to speak, but I capture her lips in a kiss. My tongue strokes against hers the way I long to stroke my stav into her channel. She moans into my mouth as I cup her breast, gently rolling the peak between my thumb and forefinger until she is writhing in my lap.

My stav lengthens and extends from my mating pouch. Her warm, wet heat seeps through the thin scrap of fabric that separates me from her core.

She gasps as I extend my claws and carefully slice through her bra and underwear so they fall from her body.

I groan as she grinds her hips against mine and her slick folds envelop my length. I have never desired anything as much as I want her now.

"Tell me you are mine," I growl, rough and aroused. "For I am already yours, my linaya."

"Kaj," she whispers breathlessly between kisses. "I'm yours."

My nostrils flare again as the scent of her arousal strengthens. I am desperate to bury myself deep inside her and fill her with my seed. A burst of precum erupts from my stav, and I still. This is strange. This only happens when...

I pull back just enough to meet her eyes evenly. "How often do you enter your heat cycle?"

She blinks. "Heat... cycle?"

"Your fertile peak," I explain. "How often does it happen?"

"Once a month... every thirty days or so." Her small brow furrows as she mouths numbers to herself. She lifts her gaze back to mine. "Technically, I'm probably in my fertile window now."

CHAPTER 21

ANNA

His irises are almost completely eclipsed by black with hunger. His voice is a low and rumbling growl. "I believe I am experiencing my mating cycle, which is triggered in a male when his partner reaches her fertile peak." He dips his head to the curve of my neck and shoulder, inhaling deeply before his tongue licks my skin and he growls again. "It is driving me mad."

He pulls me off his lap and sets me on the bench beside him as he stands.

"Where are you going?"

"I must leave," he rasps. "If I stay, I will be tempted to take you."

"But I want you, Kaj. I want to be yours."

He shakes his head. "Not like this, my beautiful linaya. My need is too great. I fear I might take you roughly in my current state, and I do not want you to fear me."

"I trust you, Kaj. You won't hurt me. I'm not afraid."

He starts for the edge of the balcony, but I grab his hand, stopping him abruptly.

He spins with inhuman speed and pins my back to the wall beside the sliding glass doors. His lips are twisted in a feral snarl and his pupils are blown wide. "You must let me go, Anna. I do not wish to take you like this."

"What about what *I* want?" I ask. "I want *you*, Kaj. I love you and want to make love to you. Claim me as your mate."

He clenches his jaw, and I can tell it's taking all of his control to remain still. "You would want me as I am? You are not afraid?"

"Not of you, my love."

His *stav* is hard against my abdomen as heat pools deep in my core. I press my lips to his. When I pull back, I cup his face with both hands and stare deep into his eyes. "Claim me," I whisper. "I'm yours, Kaj."

"You are certain?" he rasps.

"Yes."

He crushes his mouth to mine in a searing kiss as he lowers me to the floor. He runs his hands up and down my body, the tips of his fingers brushing lightly across my breasts, making me arch into him. He fixes me with a fiery and possessive stare. "You are mine," he growls.

"I'm yours, my love," I agree.

He lowers his head to my chest and closes his mouth over my left breast while he cups the other. He scrapes his teeth over the already stiff peak and then begins a gentle suction against my skin that drives my pleasure to new heights.

I grip his horns as I arch up against him, wanting more. He traces his tongue down my body until he reaches my mons. His tail wraps tightly around my thigh, opening me completely to his gaze. "You are perfect," he whispers.

He guides my legs over his shoulders and dips his head between my thighs. I gasp as he drags his ridged tongue through my folds. Using his horns, I guide him to the small bundle of nerves at the top. He laves at the sensitive flesh until I'm breathless and panting beneath him.

Pleasure ripples through me with each swipe of his tongue. I'm so close; I'm almost at my peak.

He pulls back, and I whimper a protest. I was so near the edge. He moves up my body until his face is even with mine. I only have a moment to stare up at him, dazed and breathless with unfulfilled need, before I feel him notch the crown of his *stav* at my entrance.

He hesitates. "Do you accept me, Anna?"

"Yes, Kaj. I want you."

His gaze holds mine and the breath stutters from my lungs as he slowly enters me. Tight heat blooms in my core. He's so big, it's almost overwhelming. The hard ridges of his *stav* rub my channel in all the right ways, and the sensation is too much and not enough all at once.

He groans as I flex my hips against his to take him even deeper. "So tight," he rasps.

A low moan escapes me as he rocks back and forth until he's seated completely inside me. A burst of heat fills me, so intense that I gasp.

Did he come so soon? Are we done?

Disappointment starts to creep in as he begins to pull out, but he captures my gaze and strokes back into me. Judging by the expression on his face, I know we're far from done.

Another burst of heat blooms deep in my core, and I cannot help the low moan that escapes my lips at the sensation. "What is that?" I barely manage. "That intense warmth."

He wraps his tail around my thigh, holding me still as each thrust becomes deeper and more forceful. "I am claiming you," he grits out. "My biology demands that I fill you with my essence. The precum softens your womb so that when I release, your body will eagerly take in my seed."

My head falls back as the delicious sensation fills me again. Already, the small muscles of my channel begin to flex and quiver around his length as I creep closer to the edge. If that's not even his full release, I can't imagine how intense that will be.

Through the fog of my pleasure, his words suddenly hit me. I reach up and touch his face. "You'd be all right if we got pregnant this soon?" My voice is breathless even to my own ears.

Instead of answering, he crushes his lips to mine and increases his pace, each stroke longer than the last. I cling to him, feeling the strong muscles along his back flex beneath my fingers each time he thrusts into me.

"I want everything with you, my beautiful Anna," he gasps between kisses. "You are mine. Tell me you are mine, my linaya."

"Yours," I breathe. "Only yours."

He wraps his wings around my body. I dig my nails into his back and wrap my legs around him; it's all I can do to hold on as he pumps into me.

My toes curl with pleasure as his strong body moves over mine. His gaze holds mine, full of fire and possession. "You are mine," he growls. "And I am yours."

Warmth erupts deep inside me, followed quickly by a second burst. I never knew making love could feel like this. Pleasure ripples through me as I try to arch into each of his thrusts. I'm so close. My entire body goes taut like a bowstring and then my release roars through me, flooding me with overwhelming desire.

Wave after wave of pleasure moves through me, and just when I think it's over, he cries out my name as his stav pulses deep inside me.

I'm flooded with delicious and intense heat, sending me

spiraling into another orgasm even stronger than the last as he roars out my name above me.

He collapses on top of me, carefully balancing most of his weight on his elbows to keep from crushing me beneath him. He skims the tip of his nose along mine then presses a tender kiss to my lips. "You are mine," he whispers. "My linaya."

I smooth my hands down the length of his back, enjoying the feel of his body over mine, his *stav* still hard inside me. "Yours, my love."

I'm surprised when his tail curls around my thigh and pulls my leg over his hip again. A soft moan escapes me as he restarts his slow, steady rhythm. "Already?"

A smile tugs at his lips. "I've heard your human males need time to recover after they release. I do not. I will take you several more times tonight."

His name escapes my lips in a breathless whisper as his strokes grow long and deep. I know we're not going to get any sleep tonight.

~

When I wake in the morning, his arms and wings are wrapped around me. My body aches slightly between my thighs, reminding me that I've been thoroughly claimed by my mate.

He opens his eyes and gives me a sleepy smile before nuzzling my hair.

"Good morning, my love." I place my palm to his chest, directly over the glowing fate mark pattern.

He covers my hand with his, his gaze gleaming with love and devotion. I shift to snuggle closer but wince as a small twinge of soreness moves through me.

His eyes flash with concern. "Are you all right? Did I hurt you?"

CHAPTER 22

KAJ

P anic coils tightly in my chest as I wait for her answer. Because of my mating heat, I took her roughly instead of tenderly as I should have. "Forgive me, my linaya. I should have been more gentle last night. I—"

She puts her finger to my lips, silencing me. "You don't have to apologize. Last night was wonderful. I'm just a bit sore, that's all."

I unwrap my wings from around her form and scan her body. She is so perfect and yet so fragile, my delicate mate. I trace the tips of my fingers lightly across her petal-soft skin. I thank the gods that she allows me to touch her so intimately—that she has accepted me as hers.

Flaring my nostrils, I inhale deeply of our combined scent. Her inner thighs are covered in my release, and I long to take her yet again. However, I must bring her something to eat first. My mate requires sustenance. I will gladly perform my duty to provide for the one I treasure more than anything.

She covers herself with a robe before we go downstairs. While I dislike that she hides her beautiful form, I am pleased that only *I* am allowed to ever see her without clothing.

While we wait for our meal to heat in the warmer, a sharp cry sounds from the corner of the room. It is Callie.

My mate rushes toward her. "What's wrong, Callie?" she asks as she extends her palms toward the obviously distressed camali.

I look down and notice she is sitting on eggs, where there were none earlier. A sharp crack slices the air as a thin line forms in one of the shells.

"Look." I point out the egg to Anna. As if Callie understands what I am showing my mate, she moves off her eggs and watches them expectantly.

Anna blinks up at me. "She laid eggs?"

I nod. There are three total, each a different shade of blue.

We watch in wonder as the first shell cracks open and a tiny face appears. Immediately, Callie begins cleaning the fledgling, licking its entire body from head to tail. When she is done, she carefully clamps her jaw around the back of its neck and offers it by its scruff to Anna.

I gape. This is a rare honor. Camali are highly intelligent creatures. Callie is offering her fledglings to my mate because she knows we will protect them, demonstrating a familial bond of sorts.

Anna looks at me. "Should I take it?"

"Yes. She is showing you that she trusts you."

Anna takes the small creature from Callie. As she cuddles the fledgling in her palm, its tiny wings expand and flutter against her skin. "You're so cute," she coos.

After all the eggs have hatched, my hearts clench as Callie

offers my mate the last two. With three tiny camali in her arms, Anna beams, humming a soothing tune.

The sight makes me imagine her holding our fledglings. Of course, that leads me to remembering us making love. My stav hardens in my mating pouch and I realize that my mating heat is far from over.

Anna returns all the tiny camali to their mother then turns back to me. "Can we keep them?"

How can I deny her anything? "Camali are not only intelligent creatures, they are excellent guard animals. If you wish, my linaya. We will add them to our family."

I'm rewarded with a smile that stops my hearts momentarily.

"But I must warn you, most camali are solitary creatures that do not like to share their territory. Most camali females only keep their young close until they are weaned. Then they chase them from the nest."

She casts a sorrowful look toward the fledglings. "How terrible to be chased away by one's own mother."

I wrap my arm around her. "It is their nature."

I cannot deny that I am pleased to see the maternal instincts my mate has already developed toward these tiny creatures, supporting my belief that she will be an excellent mother to our young.

"Come," I tell her. "Let us eat."

She nods and we take our meal to the balcony.

As we eat, all I can think of is pulling her into my arms again. When she is finished with her meal, I curl my fingers reflexively into my palms as a distraction. I want her—badly —and I long to sheathe myself deep inside her. Despite our mating last night, I still need her to be the one to initiate contact. I want her to feel safe and in control. The last thing I want is to trigger a painful memory.

She stands and approaches me with a half-lidded gaze.

She stretches onto her toes and twines her arms around my neck. "What are you thinking, my love?"

Clenching my jaw, I lose the fight to keep my stav from extending from my mating pouch. It presses insistently against her abdomen. "I want to sheathe myself deep inside you and fill you full of my seed until you can take no more," I grind out, my voice rough even to my own ears. "But I do not want you to fear me."

She smiles against my lips. "I'll never be afraid of you. Ever."

She reaches between us and wraps her fingers around my stav. Gently, she strokes my length, and a low growl escapes me.

The last of my control falls away, and I scoop her up into my arms and carry her into the bedroom. We only make it as far as the sofa. I am so desperate to be inside her, I lower her feet to the ground. She turns to position the pillows for us to lie down, presenting me with a tempting view of her backside.

How can I resist such delicious temptation? I dip my fingers beneath the hem of her robe and slide the fabric off of her, baring her lovely form to my gaze. Pulling her back against my body, I dip my head to the curve of her neck, pressing a series of kisses along the delicate flesh and tasting the sweet salt of her skin.

I long to touch her everywhere, relishing the feel of her bare skin against mine. The soft mounds of her breasts call to me and I cup them, gently teasing the peaks between my thumb and forefinger as she writhes beneath me. She moans and arches her back. A small burst of precum erupts from my stav and runs down her inner thigh.

I move one hand further down her body to her feminine place. When I run my fingers through her delicate folds, I find them already slick with arousal. A dark and primal instinct unfurls from deep within, demanding that I take her. Now.

I smooth a hand over her back, guiding her forward over the plush arm of the sofa. She looks over her shoulder at me, her eyelids heavy with lust. I position the crown of my stav at her entrance and push forward. A series of breathless moans escape her lips with each roll of my hips as I slowly enter her. I sheathe my stav deep in her warm, wet heat. She's so tight, I groan as the muscles of her channel flex and quiver around my length.

My hips push into her soft and giving backside. I am already addicted to my mate. The pleasure is intense, driving my thrusts to quicken and deepen.

Pinned in place, she writhes beneath me. I lean forward, covering her with my body. I wrap one hand around her hip, and band my other around her to cup her breast, holding her in place while I thrust into her from behind.

The tip of my tail reaches between us, teasing the sensitive hooded flesh between her thighs that makes her entire body light with pleasure.

I love all the sounds she makes as I stroke deep inside her. She moans loudly then releases a keening cry as the small muscles of her channel clamp down around my length and she finds her release.

It triggers my own, the force so great I roar her name as my essence erupts from my body, filling her with my seed.

I remain inside her but pull her into my arms and gently lower us to the floor. Panting heavily, she reaches back for me, guiding my lips down to hers. "That was amazing," she whispers. "How could I have waited so long to make love?"

My stav twitches deep inside her, releasing another burst of precum that makes her mouth fall open with a gasp.

"Oh Stars," she murmurs. "*Mmmm. Feels so good.*"

I trail my hand down her waist until I reach her folds. Her

inner thighs are sticky with our combined release and I inhale deeply, relishing that she is mine.

We mate so many times during my mating heat I have lost track of time. I cannot get enough of my mate. Each time we make love is better than the last. It is difficult to force my body to leave hers even for a moment.

She is asleep in my arms, but my stav is still buried deep inside her. I struggle to remain still for I know she needs rest.

A strange scent fills my nostrils, and I jerk my head toward the balcony. It is another Drakarian—a male. But who would come here?

Carefully, I pull away from my mate. She wakes, turning to me in concern. "What's wrong?"

"Someone is here," I tell her, stepping between her and the door. Whoever this intruder is, he will not be allowed anywhere near my mate.

"What?" She sits up and pulls the blanket from the bed to cover herself. "Who? How do you know?"

I growl. "I can scent him."

Her eyes are wide with fear as they peer into the darkness, so I move to reassure her. "I do not know who it was, but he is gone."

No sooner do the words leave my mouth than the wind carries another scent into the room. Alarm bursts through me. Several Drakarians are nearby. I hurry to the balcony window.

An orange-red colored Drakarian lands outside. I flare my wings, shielding my mate behind me. "Stay back, Anna!"

When the male's red eyes meet mine, I recognize him immediately. It is Varus's personal guard, Rakan. "Why are you here?"

He cranes his neck, trying to catch a glimpse of Anna. "We have come because you took the female. Her friends were worried. I did not believe you would take her against her will, but I heard her crying out as you were mating her roughly just now." His features twist in disgust. "How could you do such a thing? I never believed you would—"

Anna moves to my side and takes my hand. "He wasn't hurting me," she snaps. "How dare you spy on us?"

His jaw drops, but he quickly snaps his mouth shut. "But I heard you crying out as if—"

"Human women like to be vocal when we mate."

He blinks at her as if he cannot believe what she has just said. "Our females are—"

I know he probably means to tell her that our females stay silent during the mating, except for occasional growls. However, she cuts him off mid-sentence. "I'm not Drakarian. I'm human."

He bows low and when he straightens, guilt marks his expression. "Forgive me. Your friends were worried and insisted that we check on you." His gaze shifts to mine. "I did not believe you would ever harm a female, but when I came upon you while you were mating, your mate was so loud, I thought you had hurt her."

She rolls her eyes and places a hand on her hip. "Well, he didn't. So, you can report to my friends that all is well."

He smiles nervously. "You can tell them yourself. They have all come." He gestures outside.

I retrieve her robe and shield her while she wraps the fabric around her form. We head to the balcony, and I search the sky, noting all the Drakarians in flight overhead.

"You can come down," I call out. "It is all right."

"Yes," Rakan adds. "They were just mating. Very loudly."

It is difficult to suppress the smile that tugs at my lips as my mate growls at him. Her cheeks flush deep red in embarrassment and anger.

Varus and Lilliana are the first to land, followed by Raidyn and Skye, then Llyr and Talia.

My nostrils flare and I arch a brow at Llyr. He and Talia smell strongly of each other. "Are you two mated, finally?"

He wraps a possessive arm around her and grins. "Yes." The fate mark on his chest glows proudly against his blue scales.

"Are you two together now?" Talia asks.

Anna hugs me tightly and nods. "Yes. He's wonderful," she adds, and my hearts fill with pride that my mate is so pleased to be mine.

Varus arches a brow. "You should have contacted us when you left. My mate was worried for her friend."

Raidyn steps forward. "Mine, as well."

"Forgive me if I do not inform you of my every move," I snarl. "Especially when it has to do with my linaya and kingdom."

My parents land next to Varus. My mother's eyes shoot instantly to Anna. Her gaze darts briefly to my chest and the glowing fate mark, then she smiles. She opens her arms and embraces Anna warmly. "Welcome to our family, my daughter."

I swallow against the lump in my throat as my father hugs her as well. He places a hand gently atop her head as he used to do to me and my sister as children. His eyes are bright with tears as his voice quavers. "We have been without a daughter for so long. I am sorry that you will never know our Rajila. She loved her brother. Fiercely. Seeing him so happy, I know she would have loved you as well. Welcome to our family, my daughter."

"Thank you," she murmurs. "I was worried that you wouldn't like me because I'm... different."

My mother takes her hand, squeezing it gently. "As long as you both are happy. That is all that matters."

Anna leads everyone inside and down to the first floor. Lilliana, Skye, and Talia each take turns holding and cooing over the camali and her fledglings. I'm surprised Callie allows this, but when her green eyes meet mine, I recognize the intelligence behind them. She knows they mean her no harm and is more interested in the commotion disturbing our normally quiet nest.

Varus leans closer and arches a brow. "Is it safe to allow them to handle the camali so casually?"

"I am not sure it is wise," Raidyn mutters under his breath.

"I was thinking the same," Llyr adds. "Do they know that camali are highly skilled predators?"

As if in response to his question, the camali flexes its claws against Talia's arm while she murmurs loving words to the creature. But I note that Callie is careful not to puncture Talia's fragile skin.

"My cousin had one as a child," I tell them. "They are only dangerous if threatened. If anything, Callie feels oddly maternal and protective of the humans because of their small size and delicate forms."

We watch the camali roll over on the floor playfully as her fledglings surround her. Lilliana reaches down and rubs her belly, and Callie emits a loud purr of contentment.

"Yes, I believe you are right," Varus says. "But I needed to ask since I cannot take chances with my mate's safety."

Lilliana looks up at him with shining eyes. "Can we get one, Varus? Please?"

He smiles back at her and nods. "Whatever you desire is yours, my linaya."

She beams, returning her attention to the camali. He

turns to me. "You will bring one of the fledglings to us after they are weaned, will you not?"

"I, uh…"

"And us as well?" Llyr asks.

Raidyn crosses his arms over his chest. "My mate will have the first pick of the litter."

Fortunately for us, camali prefer to live in solitude. The mothers wean and then leave their fledglings to fend for themselves. If this were not truth, I would be afraid to take anything from Callie that she did not wish to part with. That is why camali make such excellent guard pets. When they form an attachment to their owner, they are fiercely loyal and would die to defend them.

I smile. "This will work out well, I think. My mate wishes to see each territory in this world. She has the heart of an explorer. When the fledglings are ready, we will bring them to you."

As Callie begins nursing her young, our mates return to our sides.

Skye hugs Raidyn and smiles up at him. "I think I want the gray-striped one because it reminds me of you, my love."

He darts a glance at me, and I nod in understanding. He wraps a possessive wing around her. "Then that is the one you shall have."

Lilliana places a hand low over her abdomen as she faces Varus. "It will be safe to have around the baby, right?"

He nods, for he knows a camali will guard them and their child with its life once it bonds with them. "Yes, my linaya."

Talia stretches onto her toes and kisses Llyr before turning to Anna. "Looks like we'll be closest to each other. Llyr says it's only an hour from here to the castle."

"Wonderful." Anna grins. "We can visit all the time, then."

Raidyn steps forward. "Varus and I have been discussing the construction of transports for our mates and the rest of the humans to use since they do not have wings. These will enable humans to travel more independently of Drakarians."

While I like the idea of my mate having easy access to my world, I'd prefer to be the one transporting her. As if reading my thoughts, she takes my hand and looks up at me. "I prefer flying with you, but it would be nice to have a mode of transport if you're busy."

I press a soft kiss to her lips as I meet her eyes evenly. "I am never too busy for you."

She gives me one of her dazzling smiles and my hearts fill with warmth.

Varus places a hand on my shoulder, drawing my attention to him. "We have also discussed restarting the tradition of the harvest games again."

My brows go up. This is indeed good news. The harvest games used to be times of great enjoyment between the Clans when warriors could prove themselves. It was also a symbol of our unity and peace amongst each other. "I look forward to restarting this tradition," I tell him.

Rakan—his guard—moves to his side. "I request permission to return to the castle of the Water Clan."

Varus nods. "Of course. We will meet you there."

Without hesitation, Rakan turns and walks toward the balcony, taking flight immediately.

I frown. "Is something wrong?"

Varus smiles. "He is eager to return to the human female he has had his eye on."

"Ah," I reply, remembering how jealous he was when I flew Holly on my back to the Water Clan territory. "You are speaking of Holly."

He nods.

"Does she return his feelings?" I ask, curious to know.

Varus arches a brow and turns to his mate—Lilly. "It is hard to tell just yet."

Lilly looks to me. "I think she does, but I guess we'll have to wait and see."

Anna wraps an arm around my waist and I curl my wing around her, pulling her even closer before I press a tender kiss to her temple. I am blessed beyond measure that this perfect female has chosen me to be hers.

Rakan is a good male—known far and wide among the Clans as one of the strongest and bravest warriors. I hope that he finds happiness like I have.

EPILOGUE

KAJ

After we've made love for the second time this morning, I reach down to brush her dampened hair back from her face as she sleeps against my chest. I move my hand to her lower abdomen and rest my palm on her petal-soft skin.

Closing my eyes, I concentrate. We have created life through our bonding—of this, I am certain. A possessive growl rumbles my chest as I tighten my wings around her. The gods have blessed me by choosing such a perfect mate.

As if sensing how much I wish to see her lovely eyes, her eyelids flutter open. She smiles sleepily. "Good morning, my love."

"Good morning, my linaya."

Callie purrs contentedly in her bed in the corner, surrounded by her fledglings. Their tiny faces peeking up over the blanket as soon as they hear us speak.

"Good morning, my loves," she hums.

They flutter their little wings and fly onto the bed, landing beside us.

We're going to keep Callie, while one fledgling each will go to Llyr and Talia, Skye and Raidyn, and Varus and Lilliana. I must admit that it will be hard to part with them, but camali are territorial creatures. Once her offspring are weaned, Callie would probably not tolerate the fledglings in our home for very long. But they are far from old enough to leave the nest yet.

Anna gets up and goes downstairs. The camali follow her because they know she will feed them. We have decided to stay in our nest a bit longer before moving to the castle. My mate claims it is not unusual for humans to vacation after bonding—she calls it a *honeymoon*.

I wait, knowing that she will return to bed soon. When she does, she lies next to me and I tug her close to my body. Her gaze grows heated, and my nostrils flare as I scent her arousal.

"Does my mate wish for me to make love to her all morning?" I tease. My tail twines around her thigh as I pull her leg over my hip yet again.

Her eyes are bright with tears as they stare deep into mine.

Worried, I cup her cheek. "What is wrong, my linaya?"

A tear escapes her lashes and rolls softly down her cheek. "Nothing, my love. I just… never thought I could be this happy… that I could ever trust someone like I trust you," her voice quavers softly. "You are more than I ever could have hoped for, Kaj. I love you with all that I am."

I press a tender kiss to her lips. "And you are the blessing I prayed for all of my life, Anna. You are my everything."

She leans in and presses her forehead to mine as she whispers. "And you are mine, my love."

ABOUT ARIA WINTER

Thank you so much for reading this. I hope you enjoyed this story. If you enjoyed this book, please leave a review on Amazon and/or Goodreads. I would really appreciate it. Reviews are the lifeblood of Indie Authors.

I have great news! The next book in series is already listed on Amazon. Chosen By The Fire Dragon Guard.

For information about upcoming releases Like me on Facebook (www.facebook.com/ariawinterauthor) or sign up for upcoming release alerts at my website:

Ariawinter.com

Elemental Dragon Warriors Series

Claimed by the Fire Dragon Prince
Stolen by the Wind Dragon Prince
Rescued by the Water Dragon Prince
Healed by the Earth Dragon Prince
Chosen By The Fire Dragon Guard
Saved By The Wind Dragon Guard
Treasured By The Water Dragon Guard
Taken By The Earth Dragon Guard

Want more Dragon Shifters? Taken by the Dragon: A Beauty and the Beast Retelling
Once Upon A Fairy Tale Romance Series

Taken by the Dragon: A Beauty and the Beast Retelling
Captivated by the Fae: A Cinderella Retelling
Rescued By The Merman: A Little Mermaid Retelling
Bound to the Elf Prince: A Snow White Retelling

Cosmic Guardian Series

Charmed by the Fox's Heart
Seduced by the Peacock's Beauty
Protected by the Spider's Web
Ensnared by the Serpent's Gaze
Forged by the Dragon's Flame

Once Upon a Shifter Series
Ella and her Shifters
Snow White And Her Werewolves

Dragon Shifter Beauty & the Beast

Inspired by Beauty and the Beast, a steamy fairy tale retelling…

Each year during the blood moon, a maiden is chosen in my village.

Bound and blindfolded at the edge of the forest, they are left as sacrifice to the beast—a man that can take the form of a terrifying dragon.

None have ever returned.

To save my sister, I take her place. And I find myself drawn to the man behind the beast. If I want to survive, I'll have to break the curse that binds him.

But what will it take to set both myself and the Dragon free?

Look for title below at your favorite retailer:
Taken by the Dragon: A Beauty and the Beast Retelling

ABOUT JADE WALTZ

Jade Waltz lives in Illinois with her husband, two sons, and her three crazy cats. She loves knitting, playing video games, and watching Esports. Jade's passions include the arts, green tea and mints — all while writing and teaching marching band drill in the fall.

Jade has always been an avid reader of the fantasy, paranormal and sci-fi genres and wanted to create worlds she always wanted to read.

She writes character driven romances within detailed universes, where happily-ever-afters happen for those who dare love the abnormal and the unknown. Their love may not be easy—but it is well worth it in the end.

Thank you for taking the time to read my book!

Please take a moment to leave a review! <3

Reviews are important for indie self-publishing authors and they help us grow.

Connect with me at:

Facebook Author Page: Jade Waltz

Facebook Group: Jade Waltz Literary Alcove

Twitter: @authorjadewaltz

Instagram: @authorjadewaltz

Email: authorjadewaltz@gmail.com

Project Universe Titles:

Found
Achieve
Develop

Bird of Prey
Scaled Heart

Failure

Project: Adapt
   Found

A failed human prototype. That's all she is…

Born and raised as an experiment, Selena's life has been filled with torture, betrayal, and distrust… but one night changes everything.

Sold, attacked, and on the run, Selena is picked up by a colony ship. Struggling to find her place on this ship and trying to understand the draw she feels toward two alien males, her already uncertain life becomes downright unimaginable when she learns new life is growing inside her.

Terrified her captors will find her and take her and her children back to a life of horror and captivity, she must learn to trust her saviors, and herself.

With the help of her two mates, Selena will fight for her freedom—or die trying.

Found is the first book in a space fantasy alien romance series which will have the heroine travel through the galaxy, experiencing new things and meeting multiple aliens along the way.

Order NOW!

Other Series Cowritten w/ Aria Winter:

<u>Elemental Dragon Warriors - Alien/Dragon Shifter Romance - MF</u>

Claimed by the Fire Dragon Prince

We set out from Earth in search of a new world. I never thought it would end with us crashing on a planet full of dragon shifters.

When I'm taken from my people by a fierce Drakarian warrior, my first thought is of escape. Varus is the Prince of the Fire Clan. He claims the glowing pattern on his chest means that I'm his fated one—his Linaya.

I doubt he's going to just let me go. But what does it mean to be fated to a dragon?

Read Now!

<u>Cosmic Guardian Series - RH</u>

Charmed by the Fox's Heart
Seduced by the Peacock's Beauty
Protected by the Spider's Web
Ensnared by the Serpent's Gaze
Forged by the Dragon's Flame

Printed in Great Britain
by Amazon

59903273R00111